# ANOTHER
# TIME

# KATHRYN
# SHAY

# Praise for Kathryn Shay's novels

*"Kathryn Shay writes some of the cleanest prose around, and it's my belief she'd make the Yellow Pages sound interesting if the phone company put her on staff. And Ms. Shay knows her way around a steamy love scene."*

The Romance Reader

*"Shay does an admirable job with a difficult subject, writing…with sensitivity and realism and without shying away from any of the hard issues."*

Shelley Mosley Booklist

*"What a great book. Controversial subjects handled in a sensitive and yet honest way – characters that just walked off the page, real and warm. The story just kept coming. A heart toucher, about problems with no easy solutions. Wonderful! Don't miss!"*

A Reader

# ANOTHER TIME

### By KATHRYN SHAY

# PROLOGUE

ALISHA WATCHED AS David Ryan smiled benevolently at the two couples standing before him in the splendor of the Lansings' garden. Flowers grew from in the ground, and the entire area around him was a mass of summer blossoms. Nature still boggled her mind.

"Will you, Lucas Cromwell, cherish Dorian, love her and care for her, during your time together?"

Contrary Luke grinned at the same time his eyes filled. "I will. Oh, I will."

"Dorian Masters…" David asked the same question and she answered, "With all my heart."

Smiling still, David turned to Alex Lansing. Alex's face was already wet with tears, and he could barely respond to David's query. Finally, he muttered a yes. Celeste, looking up at him, scrubbed her hands over her cheeks, then took her vows solemnly. When she finished committing herself to him, she glanced over his shoulder. Her new family looked on, their faces alight with joy. The older one, Maddy, wore a dress similar to Alisha's—pink, Celi's favorite color, though Celeste's was darker and more fitted than the girl's. Both boys were clothed in suits, like Alex and Luke.

Celeste finished, "And I promise to cherish, love and care for you three with all that's in me."

The smallest youngling, Cody, pumped his fist in the air. "Yes!" he said, and everybody laughed.

David confirmed them married for life, and the couples kissed. Enthusiastically. Glancing at Alisha, David winked. She'd come to like the pastor and, in some ways, depend on him for his clear thinking and generous spirit. Especially since she was alone in the world…

*What will you do now, Lisha?* David had taken to the nickname, too.

*I have no idea.*

*Come back to New York. We all want you there.*

Jess and Helen, in attendance along with Alex's parents, reiterated the notion several times. *Stay with us, at least for a while,* Helen coaxed.

She'd agreed. *What will I do with my time, David? Now that our tasks are completed.*

*We'll find something for you.*

When he said the words, she'd been disturbed by the use of *we*. Though she liked him, she didn't want to get too connected to David. To a minister. Alisha was the ultimate atheist. Though she'd made a myriad of adaptations to this era, believing in a god wasn't going to happen.

She was distracted from her thoughts of the past when the ceremony ended. Everybody hugged—something Alisha accepted from the women but still couldn't get used to from the men.

A sudden wave of sadness swept through her. Would she ever, truly, become accustomed to this world? She knew now she had no choice. Originally, she'd hoped that the rest of history might have stayed the same or similar enough so that someone, perhaps Rhea, would find the record of their mission. It was possible that only those two threads—the ones involving Jess and Alex—had been pulled from the fabric of time. Though they'd been told by the Guardians that they'd most likely never be able to return to their time period, Alisha was wishing for another outcome.

But after they'd destroyed Alex's research, no one from the future had appeared to announce society had developed differently, but they remembered the women's assignment and the three of them could go back to their time. She'd clung to the notion, but now, nearly three weeks after their tasks were done, all hope was dashed.

As people gathered to congratulate the newly wedded couples, David approached her. "You're sad," he said, studying her face.

It unnerved Alisha that he could read her so well. "Why would I be sad? I love Celi and Dorian. They've found happiness."

His hazel eyes filled with understanding as they sparkled in the sunlight. "You're not alone, you know."

"Of course not. I still have Dorian in my life, especially now that I've moved back to New York. And Jess and Helen."

"And me." Just then, his phone vibrated. "I'm sorry, I have to take this."

Alisha wondered who would be calling David during the ceremony. A woman? She knew he'd dated, that archaic custom that still—what was the idiom?—winded her mind. Briefly, she wondered what kind of woman he preferred.

He returned quickly. Now his features were strained.

"Is everything all right?"

"I'll tell you later. I don't want to spoil the day."

Grasping on to his arm, she drew him farther away from the picture taking. "I won't say anything. People of your time feel better sharing things."

As if he couldn't help himself, he blurted out, "There's been another church fire. One of my minister friends was hurt. Honestly, this confirms someone in Brooklyn is torching churches."

Alisha could believe it. From her research on religion of today, she'd found that a lot of unbalanced people used this god they loved as an excuse to hurt others.

Which was another reason to reject the notion. Still, she liked David. "I'm sorry. I hope he's all right."

"She."

"What?"

"The minister is a she. Kerry Mackenzie. I know her well."

Huh! Alisha wondered why the notion of his female friend bothered her.

# CHAPTER 1

"HEY, JOEY, NICE to see you. Sorry it's under these circumstances."

The dark-haired arson investigator grinned at David. "Me, too, bro."

In a sense, they *were* brothers. They'd been in the Middle East together—Joe Destino as captain of a company consisting of two hundred soldiers and David as their chaplain. They'd seen horror and brutality that, if you thought about it too much, would knock you on your ass and keep you there.

"How many people are coming tonight?" Joe asked, nodding to the group assembling in the church's fellowship hall. A week had passed since the second fire and the wedding. Two cases of church arson in just over a month warranted investigation, at least, from the professionals. A single church catching fire could be seen as merely unfortunate. Two made them a pattern. Since he knew Joe, David had set this meeting up to discuss the situation with the other ministers.

"There are twenty in the Brooklyn ministerial group I belong to. My guess is they'll all be here."

Just then Kerry Mackenzie hobbled into the room. To Joe, David said, "Excuse me a minute."

Crossing to his friend—and sometimes lover—he greeted her with a warm hug. It made him realize how long it had been since they were together. "Ker, I'm surprised to see you here."

"I have more invested in this discussion than most of you." She'd been in her office at First Universalist Church when the fire had started. A beam had fallen on her leg as she tried to escape the blaze.

"Of course you do." He squeezed her shoulder. "I wasn't sure you'd be strong enough to come out."

She gave him a feminine smile. Her brown eyes twinkled at him. "I might need help to my seat. My leg's healing" — she stuck out the casted one — "but I'm not going to be playing tennis the rest of the summer."

Frequently, they shared a game. "Sorry about that."

As he escorted her to a table, he thought about how their relationship seemed to flare up and die down at odd times. They were in a down period, and if David hadn't been so busy with the Sisters of Doom this past four months, he would have been lonely. Kerry's pixie face and short, strawberry-blond hair was appealing, and he'd been without sex for a long time. For some reason, he thought of Alisha, who'd had no access to their SexLine, the damn thing in the future that reduced sexual encounters to clinical hookups, arranged online.

Five minutes later, David did a quick head count and signaled Joe, up front, to start.

"Hi, everybody." Joe's tone was friendly but professional. "I'm Captain Joe Destino, head of the FDNY arson-investigation division. My office was alerted when the second church fire occurred in this area, and I took over from the guys in Brooklyn when the cause was determined as incendiary."

A buzz went through the listeners. Assigning a top guy from the humongous FDNY was a big deal.

"The fires were started intentionally. We have evidence that each church was broken into through a window and found the same footprints outside each entry point."

"So both were definitely arson," the minister over at the Presbyterian Church confirmed. David liked him.

"Yes. We also found a variety of gasoline-soaked rags, a gas container and smaller cans, that probably held more accelerant, at the scenes of each one."

"This is a hell of a thing." Hal Hanson, an older guy who'd helped David adjust to life in the world when he first came to New York, made the statement.

Kerry spoke up. "Do you have any clues who the arsonist might be?"

"We're tracking some leads down now. Arsonists are usually men; juveniles are the most common offenders. Other motives are vandalism, insurance fraud, revenge—including grudges, real or imagined—and sometimes, they're set to cover up a crime."

Somebody called out, "David, you still meeting with those hooligans?"

No one laughed. Reverend Ken Banks wasn't joking. Of all the pastors here, he was the most difficult to get along with because of his biases. David prayed for him. "I still meet with a group of teenage boys biweekly. We shoot some hoops when the weather's nice. Have supper together. Talk about things. But I'd never call them hooligans."

Joe cocked his head. "I'll need to speak to you about them."

The notion didn't sit well, but he tried not to prejudge his friend.

Another woman spoke up. "People blame religion for screwing them up. Since I think that's sometimes the case, you should pursue that motive."

For the next hour, they bantered with Joe about the reasons this might be happening to them. Then he gave them more information on taking precautions: try not to be alone at church, make sure entries and windows are extra secure, watch for strangers hanging around. The group finally broke up about eight.

David was cornered by Ken and after a few minutes, Kerry approached him. "Would you help me to my car, David?" she asked.

"Sure. We'll stay in touch, Ken."

As she linked her arm with his, Kerry whispered, "I thought you might want a reprieve from the Dark Ages."

David was a minister and tried not to think unkind thoughts about someone, but he *was* human, so he chuckled. "Thanks. How a man of God could hold such backward views is beyond comprehension."

Walking out into the warm night, David took pleasure in the balmy evening. They'd just reached Kerry's car when another vehicle drove into the parking lot. He didn't recognize it and watched as the driver parked then got out.

Ah, Alisha Law.

• • •

ALISHA STOOD BY her vehicle, definitely out of her comfort zone. She rarely doubted herself, but earlier, she'd been plagued by philosophical questions as she sat at her computer in Jess and Helen's lower level: Why was she here now? What was she to do? Thinking about that made her restless, something people of her time rarely experienced because they were so busy trying to survive and keep society functioning. Now, seeing David standing with a woman, her unease escalated.

Of course he had a female friend. She was wrong to come to the church unannounced, expecting him to be available. She reached for the door handle of the Prius—which she'd been forced to purchase out of necessity—to leave.

"Alisha, wait." David's face wreathed in smiles as he walked toward her. Grasped her hand. "What a nice surprise."

Still not accustomed to men touching her outside of joining, she fought the urge to disengage from him. "I should have called." She nodded to the woman with hair the color of Helen's. "You're busy."

"I just finished up. Come meet Kerry."

Oh, great. "No. I'll return another time when you're not with someone."

He tugged on her hand. She thought about resisting, but she let him lead her to the sporty car where this Kerry still stood. Really, the woman should own a hybrid or another more environmentally friendly vehicle.

"Kerry, I'd like you to meet my friend Alisha."

The woman smiled generously. She was another delicate one, again like Helen, slight of stature, no muscles to speak of.

"Hello." Alisha nodded to the woman's leg. "You're injured?"

David put his hand on Kerry's shoulder in a familiar gesture. "Kerry's the pastor who was hurt in the last church fire."

"Oh, I seek you…I'm sorry to hear that. Did your church sustain damage, also?"

"I'm afraid so. Plans are under way to clean up and restore, but we can't have services there." She gave David a very feminine smile. "David's offered his church to us in the interim."

Of course he had. Outside of Celeste, David was the most generous person she knew.

The woman checked her timekeeper. "I have another meeting soon. Nice to meet you, Alisha." She took David's hand, squeezed it, said, "Call me," and got in her car, drove away.

"I didn't mean to interrupt."

"That's all right. The fire investigator is still here." At her quizzical look, he added, "He came to talk to our ministerial group about the recent fires. It seems there are enough similarities that show a pattern of arson." David's brown brows furrowed, visible in the still-light evening. "We're all worried."

"I can understand why."

He cocked his head. "You have no fire in your time, right?"

"Correct. All our energy derives from lecci crystals, mined by robotic devices. So there are no such incendiary devices like candles or matchings."

A grin spread across his face.

"What?"

"It's matches."

"I still get things wrong."

"Not much." He gestured to the church. "Come on, I'll introduce you to Joe Destino, the captain."

The thought of her earlier feelings of loneliness, the hollow in her heart caused her to go with him. He opened the door to the side of the church called a fellowship hall. Another of their sexist terms.

The last of the ministers were leaving. David bade them good-bye then he and Alisha approached Joe, who was packing up his things. "Hey, buddy, I'd like you to meet a friend of mine."

The man looked up. Dark-as-night eyes, muscular, compact build. Longish hair with waves in it. Her first thought was *SexLine material.*

"Must be my lucky night." He held out his hand for the odd custom of shaking. "Joe Destino."

Though it transmitted germs, she performed the ritual and gave him a smile. "Alisha Law."

He glanced at David. "Since when did you start hanging around with foxes, Ryan?"

Foxes? As in animals that were dog-like and unfriendly? Earnestly? That's what he thought of her?

"I always like surrounding myself with beauty, you know that." He winked at Alisha. "So, what next?" he asked Joe more soberly.

"We keep after leads. Hopefully, we'll find this guy before he strikes again."

David had told her most arsonists were men. The few miscreants they had in Alisha's society transcended gender.

"I'll be on my way," he told them after a bit more discussion. "I have a meeting with the fire chief." He circled around the desk, socked David in the shoulder, and rested his hand on hers — incredibly personal for having just met. "I hope I see you again, Alisha."

"Thank you." She didn't know what else to say.

"Show yourself out, buddy."

"I will."

David dropped down on one of the chairs assembled in rows. "Have a seat."

She sat across from him and blurted out, "I don't understand the fox analogy. To me, it means something negative."

"Another idiom. He meant it as a compliment."

"I deduced that from your comment." Which for some reason had pleased her. She glanced after Joe. "He's very attractive."

"Ah, stay away from Joey. He's a lady killer."

"Earnestly?"

David laughed aloud. "Sorry. He dates lots of women and breaks their hearts."

"It is still difficult for me to fathom women having close personal relationships with men."

"I know that concept is hard for you to understand. Maybe you'll come to accept it. Like it, even."

"No, I don't think so." She looked around. "This space is pleasant. It's where you gather to socialize?"

"Yep. We have coffee hours after worship services, dinners, parties here." He studied her. "You should join my church."

Stunned, it took a minute for Alisha to even emit a chuckle. "David, I know you find comfort in a being who supposedly listens to you when you talk…"

"And talks back."

"Which is even more strange. But that notion was lost when grim reality descended on the people of the future."

"So you said. The dying of religion breaks my heart."

Another idiom meaning to feel bad.

"I'm glad you have it…him…her and it comforts you. But I never could be a believer."

"We'll see about that. I'll get you to a service one day."

She didn't contradict him. Though she disagreed with him on religion, she enjoyed bantering with him about it. And David was always so upbeat she liked being around him.

"So, what can I do for you?"

"I've been living with Jess and Helen for too long. I think they need privacy, especially when the child comes." She said the latter with awe. Conception, actually carrying a fetus in the womb, expelling the baby out of your body was miraculous to her.

"Perhaps. Or you could stay and help her when the baby arrives in a few months?"

"I feel the need to have my own space. Everyone in the future values their privacy, and I've had little since we arrived. Would you help me find a suitable dwelling? I didn't want to bother Jess and Helen with this — for one thing, because they'll protest — but I don't know anyone else to ask." Another reason to feel lonely. She'd had female friends other than Dorian and Celeste in her time and had seen them regularly.

"I'd be glad to help you, on one condition."

"You'll put a caveat on assisting me?" She didn't like the idea at all.

"Uh-huh. Come to church. Just once."

"Oh, David…"

"Please."

"Fine, just once. After you assist me. And I get to decide when."

"It's a deal." He held out his hand and they shook. But he didn't let go. He cradled her hand in his. "Maybe you can make some friends at church."

She glanced toward the door. "Or your *buddy* Joe Destino could be my friend." She arched a brow. "Maybe more."

David didn't like the joke. Though he rarely voiced displeasure, she noticed his shoulders stiffened and his eyes got this certain light in them when something disturbed him.

Tonight, it was nice to have someone looking after her.

# CHAPTER 2

FROM THE CROMWELL porch, Alisha watched as Dorian and Luke exited their vehicle. Both appeared relaxed and hopelessly in love after their two-week moonhoney. She thought of Celeste's words before the wedding...

*We must stay in our time, Lisha. I know you hoped otherwise because of the miniscule probability that we could go back, but you're going to have to adapt. Open yourself to new things.*

*I learned how to drive one of those awful vehicles.*

*What about people? You have to make friends.*

*I have you and Dorian. Jess and Helen. That's enough.*

But as she watched the newlywed couple unconsciously lean into each other, touch as if they craved contact, a tiny kernel of jealousy formed inside her. The red-eyed monster. Or was it yellow? (Neither made sense.) In any case, she'd never before felt the emotion.

Spotting her, Dorian broke away from Luke and ran up the sidewalk. Alisha met her friend at the bottom of the steps and they embraced warmly. Her earlier feelings of loss combined with the relief and joy at Dorian's return made Alisha dizzy.

"It's so good to see you," she told Dorian when they drew back from each other. She eyed her, then leaned in closer. "Megadamn you for getting sex for a week straight. I *so* miss the SexLine."

Dorian linked arms with her. "We're going to have to find you a guy."

"Ditch that idea right away."

Dorian stopped. "Ditch, as in forget about. Luke's been teaching me several idioms a day."

He appeared behind Dorian and settled his hand on her shoulder. "Did I hear my name?"

With good-natured snarkiness, because that was their relationship, Alisha said, "The world doesn't revolve around you, Lieutenant."

He pulled her into an unexpected hug. "I missed you, too, Lisha."

In truth, she'd felt the same about the obstinate guy.

They all trekked inside to find Jess and Helen sitting on the couch, his hand on her belly. Alisha turned away from the sight. There was something about this having-a-child business that destroyed all her walls.

Jess looked up, tears in his eyes. "Hey, welcome back. You gotta come here and feel Jessica. She's doing somersaults in Helen's stomach."

A glowing Helen with a cute, little, rounded stomach grinned. "Yep, she is."

After greetings, everyone took a turn touching Helen's child in the womb. Except Alisha.

Dorian approached her. "No interest, Lisha?"

"It's not that. It's odd to touch her and feel that movement. She convinced me to once, and I found it spooky."

"I think it's lovely." She practically sang the words.

"Don't tell me you've conceived, too, like Celi."

"We aren't using birth control. But no, not as far as I know."

To get away from all the baby stuff, Alisha brewed coffee and tea—she wished like hellor Dorian wouldn't drink the unhealthy product of beans. Once they were settled in, had discussed the trip Luke and Dorian took to the Caribbean Sea, Alisha said casually, "I'd like to discuss something with you." As quickly as she could and with a tone that brooked no argument, she filled them in on her plans.

Jess vehemently shook his head. "Don't move out, Alisha. Please, we love having you here." His eyes got misty again. "If it wasn't for you, I wouldn't even..." His words trailed off. This happened every time they discussed how she, Celeste and Dorian were sent to this time to save his life. And had.

"I enjoy being in your home, but you need privacy. Some space." She stared at them pointedly. "And so do I."

"We hardly know you're here."

"Helen, please, don't fight me on this. I want a dwelling of my own. Though I prefer to rental it."

Luke said, "Dorian and I can help you look for one. Maybe located between us and Jess." Both resided in Brooklyn, about a thirty-minute drive apart.

"Thank you for the offer, but David Ryan has agreed to assist me."

"Did you ask him to do that?" The question came from Dorian.

Glancing at her friend, Alisha didn't like the look in Dorian's eyes. "Of course. Why?"

"No reason. I just thought I saw some sparks between you."

"Those sparks are emanating off you."

Helen added, "I invited David for lunch so he could visit with Luke and Dorian." The doorbell rang. "That must be him." She struggled to her feet. Even the tiny belly she sported caused awkwardness.

"Have you heard from Celi?" Dorian asked as Helen left the room.

"They're back from Hawaii. The kids are overjoyed to have them home."

"She loves her new family."

"She adores those younglings." Dorian rolled her eyes. "Oops, sometimes I still slip."

Alisha didn't really want them to forget their future language.

David entered the room with Helen. Today, he wore tight jeans and a white over-shirt. Hugs and greetings again, then David took a seat by Alisha. "Hi, there."

"Hi." She'd seen him twice to view dwellings in multiple-family buildings. They were called apartments. Neither time had she found anything that appealed to her. They all had a closed-in feeling, and since she'd come to this time period, she'd gotten used to open spaces.

"Doing well?" he asked her.

"Of course. You?"

He shook his head. "Still no good leads on the arson. I'm afraid the trail's gone cold."

"I'm sorry." And she was. She knew how bad he felt about the church fires and how fearful of future ones he was. She wished she could help.

After a friendly — and somewhat boisterous — lunch, she and David found themselves alone at the table. "I have another place for you to look at. It's half of a house. Spacious and airy." He drew the keys out of his pocket. "Want to go check it out now?"

"Sure. As soon as Dorian leaves. But David, I don't need much room."

"It's a ranch house. Small but cozy."

"There are cattle and horses there?"

He laughed at her again. "Ranch in this sense means one floor."

"Oh." She needed to study more. But who the hellor would understand that one? It made no sense. "In any case, I'll view it, but don't...hold your breath."

They both laughed at the idiom she got right.

• • •

AS DAVID AND Alisha approached the duplex, he hoped he'd made the right decision. He hadn't shown her this property right away. "Is the dwelling empty?" she asked.

"Yes. The tenants left suddenly. The wife got a job in Manhattan and they've moved to the city."

Tucking a piece of shiny, light brown hair behind her ear, revealing the fullness of her cheeks, she looked cute today in white shorts and a red-striped top. "The city is so crowded. I like the neighborhoods of Brooklyn."

"Me, too." He unlocked the door and they stepped inside. The smell of cleaning fluid stung his nostrils. But the lemony scent beneath it was pleasant.

The foyer opened up into a large room. Its floor and ceiling were made entirely of wood. As she peered up at the ceiling—higher than most she'd seen so far—she shook her head. "I still can't get used to the wood."

David felt sad, as he often did around this woman. "I'm sorry we've been so careless, Lisha. Hopefully, our society will do better this time around."

"I don't want you to feel bad. I hope things change, too." She waved to the room. "It's very spacious. My whole dwelling in my time would fit in here."

"The dining area is right through that archway, and next to it, a kitchen and laundry room."

She scanned the many windows. "So much light. When the far windows open there must be a lovely breeze."

Knowing how much all three women loved the outdoors, he said, "Let's try it." He walked to the broad expanse of glass in the front, pulled away the sheer curtains, and slid the panes back. When he turned, he saw she'd done the same with those on the opposite wall in the dining room. Warm air invaded the cool house, but the breeze that blew felt good.

"I like the real air better than the conditioned air."

"You'd get a lot of fresh air with these babies."

She was staring out the back, which was his favorite part of this location. "Oh, look, David. There's a deera in the woods. A deer. And, oh—a fawn."

"Amazing, isn't it?" He came up behind her. "Again, I'm sorry you had no real animals in your time."

"I'm stunned every time I see one, especially these in the wild."

The kitchen was small to him but huge to her.

The two bedroom were spacious, the bigger one with another view of the woods.

"Two bathing rooms?" she asked when they checked them out. "Why would I need two?"

"One for you and one for guests."

She leaned against the counter and reiterated, "I don't require all this space."

"Alisha, the place is not that big."

"To me, it is." She smiled. "But I love the windows, and the woods and the breeze."

They walked back out to the kitchen and he gestured through the doors. "There's a nice glassed-in porch off the back."

Peering out another big window, she craned her head. "I don't see a porch."

"It's at the very end. Built off of the other half of the house. From here, there's outside access to it."

"I wouldn't want to use someone else's porch. But there's that beautiful stone area right behind this dwelling. I could sit out there."

He hesitated, but he had to tell her. "You'd be able to use the glassed-in porch."

"Repeat please."

David took a deep breath. "Alisha, I own this double house. Both units."

"Earnestly?"

"Yes. What's more, I live on the other side of the duplex."

• • •

"BLESSED LORD,

I know the existence of Satan is why you've called me to do your work with fire, with the embers of hell. I know that, through me, you will punish the wicked and reward the good. Thank you, Savior, for allowing me to be a part of your grand plan. I understand places of worship have become tainted. I understand churches must be razed and built back up by you. Give me the strength and courage to follow your commands.

Your loyal Servant, always."

• • •

ALISHA COULDN'T SLEEP the night David invited her to live in his house—separate from him, of course. The concept was both appealing and anxiety producing. Did she want proximity to him? No—because closeness with men made her uncomfortable and edgy. Yes—because he was such a nice guy. Alisha knew she could be abrasive and being around him made her…softer.

And she liked debating religion with him. Unbeknownst to him or the others (except for Dorian who saw the tomes she'd taken from the library in Virginia), Alisha had been devouring chips...*books* and studying the religions of the Ancients up until this time period. She was searching for answers: why had society lost its belief in god, and why did people cling so badly to religion today?

Calling up the latest notes she'd taken on a series she'd found online under the search topic, The Future of Religion, she scanned them. She made it a practice to jot down her own notes on everything she read, analyzing the points in a journal.

*Six predictions for the future of religion:*

1. *Sectarianism, an obsessive devotion to a particular sect, will become more pronounced.*

That had happened before the cyber wars and chemical warfare. In the twentieth and twenty-first centuries, members of society had become fiercely Catholic, Muslim, Buddhist or Jewish. Why, though?

2. *People will no longer accept the authority that most religion asserts. They will think more for themselves and this will lead to a demise of religion.*

That happened to the Catholics. By the end of the twenty-third century, there was no Pope, no Rome, no dominance of the High Church.

3. *The patriarchy that is the core of many religions will contribute to its demise.*

This one still astounded her. Today, many people believed men and women were not equal. In her time, there was complete and utter equality, not only between men and women, but among all sexual orientations, races and social strata. All had to contribute to society to survive.

4. *Social networking will bring people of the same religion together.*

Again, this did happen in the early twentieth and twenty-first centuries. Eventually, though, all religions began to die out, despite the improvements in technology that gave people even more remote access to each other.

5. *Religion will decline when people put their faith in science and technology.*

Unfortunately, society had done this. And to a very bad end. Technology had wreaked havoc in the years preceding the creation of the Domes, and scientific research, aka Alex Lansing's work, had caused sterility. By the twenty-fifth century, much of that *progress* had been reversed, rightfully so.

6. *Given the tenuousness of life (disease, natural disasters and accidents), people will turn more to God.*

How wrong this prediction was! The exact opposite had occurred because no one could answer the question, How could a good god let such atrocities occur?

Alisha yawned and glanced at the clock. Midnight. The house slept and she should, too. But contact with David always made her come back to her research. He was smart, insightful and open to everything. When he found out who they really were and what their mission was concerning Jess, he'd easily accepted Alisha's explanation as to why they'd come to this time period. If *he* believed in this deity, was he correct?

And did it matter in regards to moving into the duplex? Probably not. Even more restless now, she left her room and walked outside through the basement exit. Still in her short nightclothes made of cotton—she'd never get used to natural fibers—she sat on a chair and looked up. Each time she did this, the stars were breathtaking to her. She'd seen them reproduced in her time's planetariums, but the fake ones didn't quite capture how the real bodies of light twinkled and seemed to wink at you, how they faded in and out. How brightly they shone.

Alisha's heart clenched. She would acclimate to this time period and hope hers and Dorian's and Celeste's actions had given the future some of those stars.

Maybe she *would* move in next to David, seek his help in becoming more settled. Maybe he could also help her find some life's work that was meaningful and contributed to society. That had been the orientation of all people in the future. There was some altruism in existence today, too, though not as widespread. She'd just have to discover what suited her.

Having made her decision, she stood and went inside. She fell asleep with visions of stars in her head.

# CHAPTER 3

SOMETIMES, ALISHA COULDN'T believe how well Dorian and Celeste had acclimated to this time period, doing tasks endemic to it. Because of her pregnancy, Celeste had taken the train from Virginia to New York to visit them. Alex was unable to drive her because he'd started work teaching Ethics Studies at a local college. Many good things had come out of his choice of a new profession, like the course he was proposing about society's ethical responsibility to future generations. The job as professor also gave him more free time to spend with his family than his research work had.

When Alisha told them she'd rented half of a house from David, Celeste and Dorian insisted they go shopping for furniture with her. As they walked through a sprawling store in Brooklyn possessing many goods for a home, they passed a mirror. "Stop," Celi said.

Alisha and Dorian halted.

"Look at us."

All three stared into the glass. Alisha had never noticed the difference in their appearances. Dorian was the tallest, most statuesque, with her toned muscles and erect posture. Her dark hair had grown longer, like Celeste's, and she pulled it off her face in what was displeasingly called a ponytail.

Celeste, willowy and seeming fragile as ever, had pretty auburn hair and slim lines.

Alisha, who matched Celeste's height and was the sturdiest. There was nothing fragile about her. "Look, Lisha. You're hair's getting lighter." Even in their time, it had been a lighter brown than theirs.

"From that lovely sun above," Dorian told her. "My color has not changed."

"Because it's so dark." Alisha stared at her own, which she kept clipped to just below her chin. It *had* lightened. And she hadn't noticed, probably because she rarely looked in one of these glass things. "Hmm."

Celeste said, "Yours is very beautiful, multi-colored. We could go to a salon and have the stylist highlight it more. Maddy does that to her hair, though it drives Alex crazy." She grinned. "I have to sway him."

They began walking again. "I don't want to know how you sway him," Alisha groused with real frustration but deep affection.

"Alisha, earnestly, you have to get yourself a man."

"I'm fully aware of the fact that I haven't joined in nearly five months." She remembered Joe Destino's dark good looks. "Though I saw a prospect the other day."

"Not David?" Celeste asked.

"David? Godheads, no. We're friends."

"You're going to be living with him if we ever pick out this furniture."

Alisha stopped short. "No, I'm renting from him. He's my landlord."

Celeste and Dorian exchanged glances. Celeste asked, "Do you know the term?"

"Nope. You?"

"I think it comes from ancient times," Alisha explained, "when the royalty provided housing for their servants."

"Can you imagine having servants?" Celeste asked dreamily.

Angling her chin, Alisha said, "You have them, Celi."

"I do not."

"You have cleaners of your house in Virginia."

"Alex insisted. I can certainly do it myself." She put her hand on her stomach. "Though even the green cleaning products could be unhealthful for the baby."

Whenever she mentioned the child, Celeste's eyes teared with joy. Alisha felt warmth and weakness spread through her, too. They had not forgotten the awesome miracle of one of them being with child.

They started walking again and stopped at two couches in a green called sage. Alisha touched the material. "I like this color."

"Me, too." Dorian fingered the price tag, though money still wasn't an issue. Their stash of diamonds had hardly been dented. "Oh, wow! Lisha, look. The tag says this is a new kind of sofa. The cushions are made to conform to the body. They actually use the word."

For some reason, that disturbed Alisha. It meant that society was well on track to build the furniture of the future, which literally conformed to the user's shape. What if they hadn't changed the bad parts?

Celeste touched her. "What's wrong?"

She told them her concern.

Dorian shook her head. "I still hold that time is a continuum and threaded with streams. If you pull out one, the others remain the same. We should be seeing signs of the development of some parts of the future we knew."

"I suppose."

"Let's concentrate on shopping," Celeste suggested. "If you get these couches, an accent chair and a rug for the big room in the front, all you'll need is a video box."

Alisha frowned. "I am not purchasing one of those."

Celeste asked, "Why? We have two."

"I don't need one. I can get all my information off my computer and computeller."

"All right. Then, on to the bedroom furniture." Celeste winked at Dorian. "We'll find a wonderful bed to *join* on."

"Ha! If that ever happens."

After three hours, they'd chosen enough furniture for the house and some for the outdoor patio. Celeste insisted they visit another store to buy accouterments for the kitchen, even though Alisha balked. She was still using the supplements, though *those* had dwindled dramatically. She partook of real food with others — the blandest she could find — but she never cooked when she was alone. Still, the concept of creating meals wasn't unappealing.

After the last purchases, Alisha put a halt to the shopping. "I'm done with this conspicuous consumption for today. Nord, people really don't need this *stuff* nor as much space as I have."

"Then why'd you move in there?"

"Because I need independence and solitude. Not things."

"Won't you be lonely?" Celeste asked.

"No, of course not. Though I want to find some life's work soon."

It was one of the first times that Alisha had lied to her friends.

• • •

DAVID'S DEN WAS located in the front of the house, next to his door to the duplex. At his computer, he reworked the church finances once again. There simply wasn't room in this year's budget for computers for the youth. Turning, he faced the picture of God on his wall. Silvery, in the vague pattern of a starburst, he'd known what the image was when he saw the painting in the art store. To him, the lightness, the way the paint shimmered, the feeling it evoked was a perfect representation of God. "So, what am I going to do?"

No answer of course. In words.

"I know, I know. You'll provide."

He was distracted by a truck pulling into the driveway. Beck's Furniture. Behind it was Alisha's Prius. She'd gone furniture shopping with Celeste and Dorian, and they must have arranged same-day delivery. He glanced at the framed picture. "I know I already thanked you for this, but I'm grateful she moved in here." Not stopping to examine why, he rose and made his way to the foyer. He opened his door just as the Sisters of Doom came to the porch. "Hi, there. Looks like a successful trip."

Celeste and Dorian had already stopped by his half of the house to say hello before they went shopping, so Celeste chattered on about their purchases, something about the couches conforming, but David was watching Alisha as she stuck her key in the lock.

"Why the scowl?" he asked her as her door swung open.

"This is too much furniture." She waved to the inside. "The space is too much."

Without thinking, he grasped her arm and leaned in. "Try to enjoy what you have. It is what it is."

She held his gaze, then nodded. That he could influence her, make her feel better pleased him. Mostly, she was too grim. He liked to think he gave her optimism or caused her to be more cheerful.

The movers struggled up the walk with a pretty green couch. David asked, "Mind if I come in and see everything?"

"Sure, you can help us arrange it." This from Dorian who took his hand and drew him inside.

They spent an hour deciding the arrangement of the pieces in the great room — with David taking Celeste's place in moving things around. When they were done, Celeste dropped down on one of the couches. "I'm exhausted and I didn't even do anything."

Dorian crossed to her. "My cue to get you home." She turned to Alisha. "Are you sure you don't want us to stay? Will you be okay?"

"I'll be fine. I'm exhausted, too, and need to rest."

David said, "I'll help with anything that's left to do."

"Don't you have to work today?" Alisha asked.

"Friday is most preachers' day off."

"I'm staying until Sunday," Celeste announced on their way out. "I'll be at services."

"Me, too." Dorian and Luke had begun attending his church. Though Dorian had confided in him that she didn't really believe in this religious jumbo mumbo, Luke did and he liked to go.

"Don't look at me," Alisha said. "I'm not coming."

David just nodded.

When he returned from walking the women out to Dorian's car — funny how all three had learned to drive — he found Alisha, arms folded across her chest, staring at the room. "If it's any consolation, this is barely enough furniture in here."

She faced him. "You know what? I'm going to try to just enjoy it, like you said."

"That's my girl." He scanned the room. "You do need to decorate your walls."

"The walls? Why?"

"The room will be more pleasant."

She rolled her eyes. "The out of inside coming in is enough for me."

"Then you'll like this. I have a housewarming present for you."

"I have heat and the beautiful stone place to build fire, though the notion frightens me."

He chuckled. "A housewarming gift is something a person needs when she moves into a new home."

She flopped down onto a chair. "There cannot possibly be one more thing I need. We bought bedding, linen, dishes and disposable products that I abhor purchasing, but I have no choice in stocking the bathing room."

"You'll like this, I guarantee."

He left her front door open and entered his side of the house. Retrieving the gift, to which he'd attached a big red bow, he brought the unwieldy present into her foyer.

When she caught sight of it, her mouth dropped. She stood and rushed to him. "Oh, David, I love it. I wanted one."

"I guessed you would."

She frowned. "But I don't know how to ride a bicycle."

"Want to learn?"

"Now?"

"Unless you're too tired."

"Suddenly I have immense energy. Let me put sneakers on." She turned. "Do you have one of these?"

"Uh-huh. I thought we could go riding as soon as you learn how."

Instead of frowning, as she often did when he suggested an activity that would bring them together socially, a huge grin spread across her face. And before she went to change, she gave him a hug—very rare for her to initiate—then left the room to get her shoes.

David shook his head. The woman had enough diamonds to buy an island, had a medical device to cure most ills and had changed the course of history, to boot, but what delighted her today was one little bike.

As he stared after her, he smiled. He very much liked peeling back the layers of Alisha Law.

• • •

ALISHA KNEW SHE was acting like a youngling about the bicycle, but as she'd told David, as soon as she'd seen the devices in action on the street, she'd coveted one. But their tasks had taken precedence over such a silly indulgence. Maybe not so silly; it was practical. Though it was unusable for long trips, she could ride it to fetch groceries, visit nearby shops and enjoy the weather, all without harming the environment. Several times she'd wondered why more people didn't choose the non-motorized device as a method of transportation.

"We'll start out back," David told her.

He wheeled the bike through her kitchen and out sliding doors of glass, over the stones of the patio, onto the grass. The sun was low but still warm, and there was a slight flutter of breeze — which messed David's hair…nicely.

"You don't ride a bicycle on the grass."

"Nope. But this is where you *learn* how to ride one. He parked the bike and jogged to the glassed-in porch off his side, which she still hadn't seen. He returned with a hat of some kind. "What is that?"

"A helmet."

She pointed to the other things he carried. "What are those?"

"Knee pads. You need them both to ride."

"I won't fall off."

"*I* wear a helmet."

"No knee pads?"

"Nope. You can forego those when you get the hang of riding." He nodded to one of the chairs she and Dorian and Celeste had purchased today, along with a round table and pretty striped umbrella of blues and greens. "Sit." He held up the pads. "I'll put these on you."

She frowned. "Don't they just slide on?"

"I want to make sure they're adjusted right." He winked. "Don't worry. I won't get fresh."

"Fresh?"

"An old-fashioned word for feeling you up."

She raised her brows.

"Touching you intimately."

Suddenly, at the thought of David *touching her intimately*, she felt warm. Stirred. She dropped down onto the chair and he knelt in front of her. She'd been too long without the SexLine if a mere suggestion of touching from this man made her blood heat. He set her foot on his thigh, took off her sneaker, slid the pad up her leg and to her knee. To prevent a shiver from his hand gliding over her skin, she said, "Oh, that was hard."

"Hush." He placed her foot inside her shoe and tied it up. The action seemed…sensuous. Then he repeated the process on the other leg, and that was even more so. When she stood, she grabbed on to his shoulder for balance.

"Feel okay?"

His hands on her felt great. "Um, yes."

They approached the bike. "This is an Electra Gypsy 3i women's cruiser bike, made for neighborhood riding. I didn't get you a racing bike because there's nowhere to ride it around here. You'd have to drive in the car to get to trails. This way you can enjoy the bike every day."

"I love the one you chose, though I don't even know what a racing bike is." She had her hand on the bars and rubbed the metal, liking its smooth steel texture.

"I also didn't get the pink one."

"Too girly for me?"

"Nah, you're plenty girly. I thought you'd like something more demure."

"As I said, I love the one you purchased. Come on, show me."

Approaching the bike, he pulled a lever and adjusted the seat to its lowest point. "You'll need the seat higher to ride, but we start out this way so your feet touch the ground." He bent down. "Now I have to take the pedals off."

"You ride without pedals?"

"Again, no, but you learn without them."

When he knelt, she noticed that, like hers, his hair had been lightened by the sun, tinting the curls with multiple shades. He made quick work of removing the pedals, then stood.

"All right. Now swing your leg through the opening and sit on the seat."

She sat. "Ouch. It's hard."

"When you're used to conformers, I'm sure it is. We can get a cover to pad it." He pointed in front of them. "The yard slopes here, so you can practice balance. Hold on tight to the handle bars, push with your feet, then lift them off the ground. Concentrate on keeping the wheels straight and your body balanced on the seat."

She pushed off the ground, the bike went forward and rolled down the incline. Fiercely concentrating on her balance, she went several yards before it stopped of its own volition.

David clapped. "Yay!" He looked like a little boy.

Secretly pleased with the tiny achievement, she bounced off the bike and wheeled it back up to him. "What's next?"

"The same thing, ten times."

"Why? I achieved the correct ride right away."

"This isn't a competition. The video I watched said ten times, so we do ten times."

"You've never taught anyone to ride a bike before?" she asked.

"Can't say that I have."

After five more repetitions, she sighed loudly in frustration. "Please, David, let's go to step two."

"I guess. The last five times, you can use the brakes. He demonstrated how the three gears worked.

She nailed that on the first time, too, but he made her complete more practices.

Feigning frustration when she insisted they proceed, he knelt down and anchored the pedals back on. Then he stood. "Stand between the pedals."

"Why?"

"For this part, we have to adjust the seat. If you sat this low, pedaling would be exhausting."

Climbing between the front and back of the bike, she stood with her legs straddling the space. He eyed the distance, then moved the lever. "Try to sit."

She did, holding on to his shoulder for balance. "It needs to be a bit higher, I think." She sounded breathless, but his hand was very close to being *fresh* when it accidentally brushed her derriere. Her mind started to spin out a fantasy of more, but she stopped it cold.

"Put the pedal at two o'clock." His voice was a little hoarse. "Place a foot on the right one—"

Having gotten the gist, she started off before he finished his instructions. Both feet on the pedals, she moved them in a cyclical fashion.

The rest, as they said in this time period, was a piece of cake. They walked to flat ground; she pedaled without a miss. He taught her how to stand and pedal faster. "That might have been a mistake," he called out when she rode too quickly on the next run and crashed into a bush. He laughed as she picked herself up. She was laughing, too, feeling carefree and young. "I'm ready for the road."

"The sidewalk, maybe." When she went back to him, he chucked her under the chin. "You look cute in that helmet, by the way."

Out front on the concrete pavement, she went slowly a ways, twice. The third time, she pedaled faster and farther. When she returned, she knew her face was animated. "David, this is so much fun. Thank you for purchasing the bike for me."

"And you can do it anytime you want." He grabbed her hand. "Promise me you won't go off the sidewalk until I can go with you."

"I promise. Can we do it now?" His stomach growled. "Oh, you're hungry."

"Yes. Contrary to you, I have to eat real food."

"I've been eating more of your real food. The supplements are running out."

"What have you eaten?"

"Some animal products for protein." She cocked her head. "And I like your potatoes."

"How about you join me for chicken cooked on the grill. I have potatoes and a vegetable."

"Which one?"

"Broccoli."

"I like broccoli. I'm not fond of brussel sprouts."

"Honey," he said hooking his arm around her shoulder. "Nobody is."

# CHAPTER 4

"RIGHT IN HERE." David opened the youth room, which was a respectable size as the church building was large, and switched on the lights. Crossing directly to the windows, he pulled them all up, then turned to face Alisha. "The computers were donated." He smiled.

Walking around the set of twelve, she inspected each. He leaned against the space between the windows. He tried to concentrate on the colorful walls the kids had painted with murals of things that interested them—like bands, locations, sayings—the thick carpeting a local businessman had paid for and the director chairs the kids used for watching movies. Anything, but look at Alisha in her skimpy top and shorts. Before he came to work, he'd caught sight of her outside on her patio, drinking tea. The air was incredibly hot today—hence the outfit—and she seemed to bask in the warm weather. Amidst the birds chirping and the sun already beating down on them, he'd walked over…

"Good morning."

Her face raised to the sun, she was grinning. "It is, isn't it?"

"Are you settling in?" It had been three days since she'd come to live in his house.

"Yes." She shook her head. "I found some of Celeste's things in a box that came to me."

"What?"

"One was full of novels about romance. I perused them. They have explicit scenes of joining outlined in them."

"So I've heard."

"But some include more than that. There are a great many based on extensive research the woman did on the professions of their characters."

"Which professions?"

"Teaching, the fighting of fires, the Secret Service. I had to look up what the last is."

"Interesting."

"You didn't come to discuss romance novels, did you?" She frowned. "This is the problem with idleness. And it's why your society collects so many *things*. People have too much time on their palms."

"On their hands. And I think you're right. But there's nothing wrong with wanting to live in a pleasant environment."

"Still, I need something to do, David."

"I'll help you find work if you do me a favor."

Her face lit. "Something in return for all you've done for us? Absolutely…"

Which is how they'd ended up here, at church, in the kids' room.

When she finished inspecting the machines, she turned to him. "Why are you happy about receiving these? From only a glance, I can tell they are primitive computers. And from a rudimentary perusal of your stores, there are much better ones obtainable."

"I know they're old. But they work, and better yet, they were donated. A congregant is closing his business. He had twelve computers to give to us." David grinned.

"That makes you happy?"

"Yeah, but I was smiling at the notion that *God provides*. I asked for a solution, and not a week later, these showed up."

"If there was really a supreme being, like you say, it would have sent more up-to-date ones." She stared at the machines, then lifted her eyes to his. "Celeste, Dorian and I have all those diamonds, David. We could buy you new ones as a thank you for all you've done for the three of us."

"I appreciate the offer, but I prefer these. We're recycling the computers, saving the planet by cutting down on over-consumption."

"Of course. Why didn't I think of that?" She sat down in front of one. Turned it on. Waited. "That took forever," she said, when it finally booted.

"Have patience. One of the few things you're not good at."

"I suppose. Everything was so imperative in the future."

"You should relax more."

"If I knew how."

"Take the yoga-meditation class one of our members teaches twice a week."

"I've read about yoga. It sounds interesting." She turned to the computer again. Clicked some keys. Frowned again. "There's not enough RAM, though that can be expanded. The motherboards are old. The keyboards stick, which is why I'm glad we talked to our computellers." She glanced up at him. "I can make them faster, update their software and fix these minor problems."

"That would be great." He pushed off the wall and walked toward her. Squeezed her shoulder. Her flesh was warm. Smooth. Silky. "I'll leave you to it," he said hoarsely. "I have a counseling appointment now then an outreach meeting."

"What kind of meeting?"

"One where we plan what we can do for others. Our church helps those in need of food, clothing and shelter by providing necessities."

She shook her head. "I still can't believe people are hungry and homeless in this time period."

"Neither can I."

He walked out the door, thinking about the future: no poverty or hunger, little crime. Everyone received an education by those trained in the fields of study. In some ways, her era was better than now. The notion intrigued him.

Reaching his office just in time to let Paul Mason in, he smiled warmly at the young vet. The man had been unemployed for eight months since his return from Afghanistan and had still not gotten through the red tape of the Veteran's Administration for his claim, a situation that enraged David. Consequently Paul had had way too much time to think about what he'd done in war.

"It's a nice day," David said smiling. "Let's go out back and talk."

They settled at the picnic table, and David smiled over at the young man. His hair was growing out and he bore a noticeable scar under his chin. He hadn't yet told David how he got it. "How you doing, buddy?"

"Take a wild guess."

"Not good. I can see it in your eyes and body language. You look exhausted. Nightmares again?" David had them when he first got back from the Middle East. His mentor, Hal Hanson, had helped with those. They came infrequently now.

"I just wish I had somethin' to do."

Alisha's line lately.

"Did you go to the job fair downtown?"

The man looked away nervously. "Um, no."

"We decided that you would."

"A buddy of mine went to the last one and said the number of vets there was depressing."

And so the conversation went. David would suggest something, and Paul would veto it. Eventually, David knew he had to take a stand. "Paul, I don't think our meetings together are working. Every week we come up with a plan and you don't follow through. I'm not sure I can help you if you ignore what we discuss."

"You're a church guy, maybe that's why." Often he made disparaging comments about the church and God. David understood why, as he'd had a lot of negative feelings when he returned too. But he'd worked them out with God.

"Would you like me to find a lay counselor for you? I know several."

"Trying to foist me off, like everybody else, Rev?"

David was taken aback by his hostile tone. "No, I'm not. You brought it up."

Briefly Paul closed his eyes. "Jesus, I'm sorry. I don't know what gets into me sometimes."

"What do you mean?"

"I get so mad at a god that mostly I don't believe exists."

David waited. When Paul said no more, he spoke. "We can work on that if you want."

"It's the last thing I want."

"Then tell me what will help."

"I don't know." A casual shrug of his shoulders, meant to discourage David.

"Let's tackle this job situation again," he suggested, ignoring the brush-off. "Start checking out local opportunities."

"The shelter people already did that."

"Let's keep trying. But you have to promise not to just blow them off."

"I can do that." He glanced to the church building. "Just nothing to do with religion, okay?"

"Okay."

David ducked inside to retrieve his computer. They worked on job searches for an hour, during which Paul got up twice, jittery for a cigarette. Finally, they'd narrowed a list to two opportunities. And David knew the owner of a diner in town that had advertised for a cook. Paul could cook. He did most of it at the shelter.

When he walked Paul back to his car, the guy turned to him. "I'm sorry for what I said about your god."

"God's yours, too."

"Nah, he forgot all about me." Paul shook his head at David. "He forgot all of us over there, Rev, even you."

Reaching out, he touched Paul's hand. "No, that's not true. I know it. But if you don't believe in God, try to have a little faith in yourself."

"Okay, I'll try."

• • •

"MEGADAMN, HOW ON earth…" Alisha played with the keys. "Unbelievable…"

The condition of the machines was worse than she had originally suspected. And she'd been distracted by David's explanation of his meeting. His church was right to help others, not because of some deity, but because it was the humanitarian thing to do. It was one of the core beliefs of her time period.

More grumbling...

A bit later, she became aware of a presence in the door-way. Glancing up, she saw Joe Destino, David's friend and the man she'd teased him about. Today, he was dressed in one of those uncomfortable-looking suit-things Luke wore; he had to be hotter than hellor, though the church was cooler than out of inside.

Joe gave her a...sexy smile. "Hello, again. Alisha, right?"

"Yes. And it's Joe, isn't it?"

He nodded. "I've been here a minute or so. Do you always talk to yourself?"

Oh, dear. Unobtrusively, she hoped, she edged the com-puteller, which she was using to update the older machines, behind a computer. She'd have to be more circumspect with it in public. "Perhaps. I've never paid any attention. I'm updating these computers that were donated but are now archaic."

"They can't be that old." He approached her and glanced over her shoulder. "I have this model."

"I didn't mean to insult you."

"You didn't. Is David around?"

"He's in a meeting."

"He said to stop by at six and we'd play some basketball." Joe gestured out the window. She tracked his gaze. Behind the church was a post with a hoop attached above a surface covered with tar. The gooey black substance was dirty, smelly and had made her gag when they'd driven by workers put-ting it on roads. She'd seen David play in that area before she left for Virginia.

"I'm sure he'll be out soon. He's been with the group for nearly two hours."

"Mind if we chat until he does?"

"No, not at all. I need a break."

And she wanted to talk to him. For a while now, she'd been thinking she might be able to help with the arson investigation, though she hadn't mentioned it to David this morning. With her skills as an observer, she might see things others didn't. She might also be able to use the computeller and spin out probabilities for identifying the perpetrator, much as she'd used it to identify the man who was trying to kill Jess Cromwell. She could never enlist the history chips to determine who the arsonist was because that would be interference, whereas using them for Jess's situation was acceptable because that was their task. She wasn't *supposed* to catch any arsonist.

The fire captain took a chair at an oval table. She stood by the wall—she'd been sitting too long—and noticed how his gaze drifted over her body. She hadn't even thought about the lack of covering these short trousers and the top without sleeves revealed. It was just so hot outside. Still, she wasn't self-conscious about his perusal, but…interested, maybe? "Is there any more news on the fires?"

"We're running down known pyromaniacs in the area. Sifting through databases."

Her computeller could make quick work of that, as well as analyze information they'd already gathered.

"What did you find out about the burn patterns and points of origin? Would commonality in those areas give you any more clues?"

"Every little bit will help." He smiled. His teeth were even and white against his complexion, which was darker than David's. "How is that you know so much about fires?"

She recalled the romance novels she'd found; there was a series on firefighters in the box. "Oh, I'm an…author. I'm writing a book about firefighters and have an arson case in it."

"Nonfiction?"

Smiling like the females on *LifeLine Television for Women* — another of Celeste's weaknesses — Alisha decided to flirt. "No, a romance novel."

His dark eyes danced and she liked the way his hair fell onto his forehead. "Now, there's a thought. Is it juicy?"

That couldn't possible mean what first came to her mind. Thankfully, he added, "Sexy?"

"Um, yes."

"If you need any help with research..."

Bingo. "You know, you *could* help me. Perhaps I could view the arson site. It would give me good details for the book."

"That's not exactly the area of research I was referring to." He gave a male chuckle. She'd gotten the double entendre, again common in this time. (Why couldn't people just come out and say what they meant?) "But sure, call headquarters." He took out a card and scribbled something on the back. "Ask to do a ride along, shadowing with me for research. I'll put a good word in for you."

"Thanks, Joe."

Again, the smile. He was *so* male. Masculine. "I was wondering—"

"Hey, Destino, sorry I'm late." David stood in the doorway. Lines of fatigue etched his face and his shoulders slumped. Alisha wondered if he was getting adequate sleep.

"No worries. Alisha is very entertaining."

She said flirtatiously, "I can be."

David's shoulders stiffened, and his eyes got that light in them that signaled his displeasure. "Let's go change clothes. We don't have a lot of daylight left."

Joe stood and faced Alisha. "Make sure you call. I can't wait to...show you around?"

David cocked his head in question.

Joe faced him. "Alisha's writing a book. She wants a ride-along with the fire department." He grinned. "I said yes."

"Of course you did," David responded in odd tone, then turned and left.

• • •

"WANT TO PLAY horse first before some one-on-one?" Joe suggested when they got out into the sultry summer air and on the hot pavement. The game entailed each player taking shots from the foul line, and when one person missed, he earned a letter in the word. The first to miss five times—and spell HORSE—lost.

"That'd be good." David didn't much care about what they played or, right now, about playing at all, as he was still thinking of the way Joe looked at Alisha. "You go first."

Positioning himself at the line David had painted on the blacktop for him and his boys, Joe set up and threw the ball to the hoop. It swished without even hitting the rim. "Your turn, old man." David was five years older than Joe. And Joe was three years younger than Alisha.

The ball left his hand, arced high and...hit the rim.

"Ha! You got an H. Try again."

*Concentrate,* David told himself. He earned an O and R before he made a basket.

When he bulleted the ball at Joe, his friend asked, "You okay? You seem distracted. Grumpy."

"I'm good. I had a disturbing meeting earlier. I guess my mind's still back at church." True, but not on Paul, as he implied.

Of course, Joe made his shot.

His next turn up, David missed twice, so Joe won the game.

"You're losing your touch, David," Joe laughed. "Want to see how you do in some real ball?"

Running a hand through his hair, David gave a disgusted snort. "Yeah, I do."

They started at the foul line, David, the loser, taking the ball first. He darted left around Joe, dribbled to the basket and made an easy layup. Returning to the foul line, he tried the same move but shifted right. Joe's reflexes were good and he compensated. So David took an almost midcourt shot, which found its target easily. "Yes! This is more like me."

They played for forty minutes. By then, with the heat still high in the end-of-summer night, they were covered in sweat. "Let's take a break."

"Yeah, I could use some water."

When they headed off the blacktop, David caught sight of the youth-room window. In it stood Alisha. She waved at them and yelled out through the screen, "Good game."

Removing bottles of water from the cooler they'd brought out, David handed one to Joe and they gulped back their drinks. The water soothed David's parched throat.

Joe nodded to the church. "Where'd you find her? She's a beauty."

"Alisha?" he asked with pretended innocence. Joe nodded. "She's related to one of my parishioners."

"Known her long?"

"About five months."

Joe chuckled. "Usually I like small, curvy women, and she's big, but boy, what a knockout."

Alisha wouldn't understand that term.

"Is she?"

"Hell, David, are you blind?"

"I guess I just don't see her that way."

Though he thought of his flirting the day he gave her the bicycle...

*Don't worry. I won't get fresh.*

*Fresh?*

*An old fashioned word for feeling you up.*

She'd raised her brows.

*Touching you intimately.*

David derailed the thought.

"Then you won't mind if I ask her out?" Joe asked.

"Out? Like on a date?"

"Uh-huh."

David hesitated. Alisha was lonely, he knew that. And she missed sex. Had been without it since she came here—at least he thought she had. David gravitated toward her—sometimes physically, a lot emotionally—but there was really nothing romantic between them. His minister's conscience told him he shouldn't decide what was best for her. "Sure, ask her out. But Joe, she's kind of an innocent in the ways of the world. Be careful with her."

Joe spit out the water he'd been drinking. "You gotta be kidding me. With a face and body like that?"

"Yeah." He'd go with their story. "She was raised by missionaries and has lived with her sisters most of her life. Both of them just got married. She's vulnerable."

"I didn't mean offense. Okay, I'll be good." He grinned a very male grin. "For a while."

With a pit in his stomach, David turned away from Joe's innuendo.

• • •

ALISHA WATCHED BOTH men start a second game of basketball. Sports were interesting. As an anthropologist, she'd
been aware of their existence in this time period—though
she'd had no idea there were so many different kinds. She
understood the psychology behind them. But in her time,
competition had given way to cooperation in order to survive,
so they'd lost the art of competing physically. She took great
interest in watching Jess and Luke play racquetball, too.

She zeroed in on Joe Destino as he leaped in front of David
and blocked a shot. He was attractive in a raw, virile way.
He'd removed his shirt, and she could see, even from here, his
pectoral muscles were sculpted, his shoulders strong. Firefighters needed to be fit.

Her gaze strayed to David. She appreciated his tall, lean
body, the graceful way he moved to the basket, the joy that
spread across his face when he accumulated two more points.
She liked him and was glad they were friends. Even if she did
feel a strange spark of...lust, maybe, once in a while for him.
Since he'd shown no sign of returning the occasional flicker—
necessary in this time period—she'd ignored her reaction.
Turning to the computers—she was only halfway through
updating them—she decided to quit for the night. She needed
sustenance and was emotionally restless.

It took her ten minutes to shut down the archaic devices.
She grabbed her pack that was carried on the back, conve-
niently called a backpack—and headed out of the room.
Intending to leave through the front entrance, she changed
her mind and traversed to the back.

They were still playing like the ancient gladiators she
knew of from the Galleries. Crossing to them, she waited until
a segment of play finished, then called out, "David?"

He glanced over. "Hey."

"I just wanted you to know, I'm leaving. I finished half of the updates, and I'll come back tomorrow to do the rest."

Holding the ball in one hand against his hip, David crossed to her, and Joe followed. Up close, both men were covered in sweat and breathing hard. She noticed how David's damp hair glistened with moisture. And of course, that other oddity: both men had hair on their chests. This was not a physical trait of males in her time. It made men today seem more…virile.

David said, "Thanks for coming in today. I'll be home in a bit."

Joe frowned. "Home?"

"Alisha moved into the duplex where I live."

"Oh." Joe sidled David out of the way. Over Joe's shoulder, Alisha could see David frown. "I was wondering if you'd like to go out some time?" Joe asked, giving her an appreciative once-over.

"Go out?"

"Yeah, on a date. With, um, me."

*Dating – a precursor to joining.* She studied Joe more closely. Once again, she noted that he was a good specimen – physically attractive, he exuded a boyish charm that David didn't have.

"I would enjoy that, Joe." She smiled at him, and again, David frowned. Didn't he like Joe? "When?"

"Are you free tomorrow night?"

"Tomorrow night is fine. Shall I meet you at a time and place?"

"Nah, I'll pick you up. I know where David lives."

She smiled. "I'll see you then, Joe. Take care." To David, she added, "You, too."

David nodded back.

As Alisha left, she wondered at David's sudden grim mood. He appeared happy most of time, but something had happened to turn that around tonight. Maybe she'd ask him about it.

# CHAPTER 5

SOMEONE KNOCKED ON David's front door. He'd been home for over an hour and was still in a pissy mood. He'd burned his supper, was tempted to shoot back some nasty emails to people who didn't deserve them, swore at the television news. And he was afraid he knew why. Unable to ignore the knock because it could be a congregant, he swore again. Dressed in only fleece shorts, he pulled open the door.

"Hi, David." She still wore the navy blue shorts and white, sleeveless top she'd had on earlier. The outfit still fit her as well.

"Hey, Alisha."

"I was wondering if you'd like to go for a walking. Unless you're too tired from the game of basketball." She shook her head. "You played like enemies."

"A walk sounds good." Maybe some quality time with her could ease the negative feelings he had about her going out with Destino. Her gaze dropped to his chest. And stayed there. Self-conscious, he said, "Let me get a shirt and shoes."

"I'll wait out here. It's a beautiful night."

"Today was a dog day afternoon, for sure."

"Excuse me?"

"When it's really hot out, we call them dog day afternoons."

"Why?"

"I have no idea."

He took the stairs two at a time, grabbed a shirt and put on his sneakers, feeling his bad mood lift. It would be fun to stroll with her in the evening.

Trundling back downstairs and outside, he found her reading her little computer thingy, which had a screen that grew to epic proportions when necessary. Immediately, she began to recite, "Dog days were when the Sirius, the Dog Star and the brightest one in the sky, rose just before sunrise. It was believed that the hot days of late summer were caused by the early rising of the Dog Star. They also believed animals went mad during this time, their wine spoiled, people became hysterical, and seas boiled. So a dog day afternoon would be one of the very hot, sticky days at the end of summer."

He laughed aloud at her penchant for research and facts. "That's thorough."

She giggled. "I'll never understand all the idioms, but I keep trying."

"You're doing fine."

Side by side, they started down the sidewalk of David's neighborhood.

"All those stars out tonight," she commented. "I miss so much about my world, but I love the natural wonders of yours."

"Your world now, too."

"I suppose."

"Lisha, would you go back to your time period if you could?"

Her head jerked around. "Absolutely. Especially since I have to believe that we've changed the bad things about the future."

"I wonder if they have religion now."

"An interesting thought. I hope there is still cooperation and closeness among the world population. Maybe it happened despite the absence of cyber wars, the pollution and the out-of-control technical progress."

"I'm amazed at what you told us. Implants in the eyes and ears."

"And a bionic hand that functioned like a computer or a cell phone."

He shook his head. "Your society was right not to resurrect so many technical advancements after the wars. It seems to go against nature."

"I agree. Luckily, so did the Guardians."

"Do you think about your world a lot?"

"When I'm idle. I enjoyed fixing the computers today."

"There are a ton of things you can do at the church. Maybe join the outreach committee. You seemed interested in that."

"I am. Helping each other is a core value of our society."

"See? You'd fit right in."

"I'll think about the committee. Just so long as you don't ask me to come to services."

"You owe me one attendance."

For a while, they walked in silence. Alisha broke it. "David, I like you a lot and I trust you. Would it be all right if I asked you some rather personal questions?"

He cleared his throat. "Yes, of course."

They passed a park at the end of the street. In the twilight, he could see there were still some children playing. "You know I have what you call a date tomorrow night with your friend Joe Destino."

David gritted his teeth. "He's a nice guy."

"You were in warfare with him?"

"He fought. I tried to offer solace."

"Your voice gets sad when you talk about those days."

"I rarely bring it up. The whole four years were horrific." He sighed heavily.

"What, specifically?"

"Choices had to made. Difficult ones. I still dream about some of mine that went bad."

Reaching out, she touched his arm. She rarely made casual contact with males but was affectionate with women. He enjoyed the contact. "I'm sorry."

"No more *I seek your forgiveness?*"

"Our phrase doesn't have the same connotation."

When they began walking again, he slid his hands in his pockets as they strolled. "So, what personal things do you want to know?"

"I'm not sure what the protocol is for dating. Celeste and Dorian didn't enter into a normal twenty-first century relationship. So I don't know how one begins, what to expect."

That shouldn't be too hard.

"And here's the personal part. What are the sexual customs of a first ritual like this?"

*Shit.*

"Okay, I'll give it a shot. Dating is whatever you want it to be. A couple goes out to a public place and talks to each other. They often share food." He frowned. "Will that be a problem for you?"

"No. As I said, I'm acclimating to your sustenance, too."

"Now *you* sound sad."

"Nostalgic, I guess."

"For pills? That's just not normal, kiddo."

She chuckled. "Continue."

"You might go to a movie or out dancing."

"You and I danced at The Mix. I liked it, except that we were trapping a miscreant." She waited. "We've been through a lot together. Thank you for helping us so much."

"God would want me to."

"Still, thanks. So after the dancing, do we return home? To whose dwelling?"

He saw a bench off to the side and thought they better sit down for this. He tugged her to it. "Either person's place."

"What happens first?"

David thought for a minute. "Sometimes people say good night on the porch. They don't invite each other inside."

"Is there any kind of sex play involved on the first date?"

*Not for you.* "It depends. Some couples sleep together right away. But I don't think it's a wise idea."

"The term *sleep together* is incorrect nomenclature."

"You better not call it joining with anyone else but me."

"True. Why isn't sex on the first date a good idea?"

"I think it's better to take things slowly. Men might get the wrong idea about you."

"They might think I'm a slut."

"How do you know that term?"

"Celi watches *LifeLine Television for Women.*"

He noticed the street lamps went on and they cast her face in an ethereal glow. "To answer your question, you'd be no more of a slut than the man would be. What I meant is joining right away sets up a different dynamic between two people."

"Do *you* wait past the first date to join when you date someone?"

Well, she said the questions were personal. "Not that there are that many women in my life, but yes, I do wait."

"How about kissing? Do you kiss on the first date?"

"Often."

Her fingers went to her mouth. "I've never been kissed."

He knew that, and the notion did strange things to his insides. "Kissing is very special."

"If Joe tries to kiss me, will he know I'm a novice? Shouldn't I be experienced by age forty?"

"Probably."

They sat momentarily in silence and he wondered what she was thinking. Right now, his mind was in places it probably shouldn't go.

"David, will you kiss me so I can get the gist of it before I go out with Joe?"

*Oh, dear Lord in heaven.* "Seriously?"

"Yes, then he won't suspect I'm different."

"Usually people kiss who are romantically involved."

"But we're friends. We like each other." She grinned. "Think of it as teaching me to ride a bike."

"I suppose I could do that."

She gestured to the spot where they sat. "Out here?"

"No. I know the people on this street. Let's go back to your place."

"On the way there, perhaps we can hold hands, another preliminary to sexual contact."

Hell. He didn't know if he should be thanking God for her offer or cursing fate.

• • •

ENERGY PULSED THROUGH Alisha as she and David reached the duplex and entered her side of the house. She was getting used to the scent of flowers she'd brought inside, the sound of the refrigerator turning on, the air filtering through the open windows. She crossed immediately into the living room, the rug squishing beneath her feet. As night had fallen by the time they reached home, she switched on a lamp situated on what they called a coffee table, though it rarely held the drink.

Turning back to him, she looked up into his face. "You're taller than Joe Destino. Will that make a difference?"

"Maybe. Your...breasts will come into contact with a different part of my body than his."

It was a nice image. "I'll figure out the angles and adjust what I'm supposed to do when the need arises."

He shifted from one foot to another. She'd never once seen David nervous, unsure or worried. "I'd say do what comes naturally, but that's not true for you." He smiled down into her eyes. "You can move a step closer."

With that, she was almost touching him. His scent rose up—shower soap and a hint of the stuff men put on their faces today. It was woodsy. She liked the woods. "Who goes first?"

"Excuse me?"

"Who initiates the contact?"

"Either person. Sometimes it happens together. Slide your arms around my neck. That way, I'll know what you want and go from there."

She started at his chest and immediately felt his muscles leap. "You reacted to my touch."

"Now that *is* normal male behavior."

Her hands traveled up to those nice shoulders, then she looped her arms around him, linking her fingers at his nape. The closeness felt good. Really good.

"At this point, I would lower my head."

"So, males begin the process?"

"You know, that used to be the case, but it's really not true today. Women start things off, too."

"You do it. So I can learn."

Holding her gaze, he lowered his head, angled it to the right. Exactly as she did. They bumped noses. "I forgot to tell you that we have to angle our heads in opposite directions."

"How do I know which direction to go in?"

"Hell, I never thought about it. Most people are right-handed and lean that way, but I'm not sure. You might just have to sense it."

"This all is pretty ineffectual, I think."

"Maybe. Now I'm going to brush my mouth against yours. Close your eyes."

"Why?"

"So you can feel more."

Soft—but firm—lips grazed back and forth over her mouth. Not being able to see increased the little stir she felt inside, but not much. From the video box, she knew these kisses went deeper.

He drew back. His eyes glimmered with emotion. "That was nice."

"Let's go further."

He cooperated. Again the gentle brush of his lips, then he grasped her arms and pressed her mouth harder with his. This was better...her skin tingled all over. She moved into him without being told to.

After a moment, he lifted his head. "Now, I'm going to open your mouth."

"With your hands?"

He laughed. "No, with my tongue."

"You can't pry open my mouth with your tongue."

His knuckles brushed her cheek. *That* felt good, too. "I won't have to. You'll want to cooperate."

"Why?"

"Because you like the kiss."

"I do."

"Um, I meant when you're with Joe."

"I hope I like it as much as this."

His brows furrowed. Without saying more, he again lowered his head, pressed his mouth firmly to hers, and his tongue prodded the crease in her lips. He was right, she opened willingly. When his tongue entered the recesses of her mouth, she felt a jolt, similar to when they first jumped through the time portal, only on a smaller scale. He kept up the action, exploring her. He seemed to *take* from her. "Put your tongue in my mouth," he whispered heatedly against her lips before he resumed the kiss.

When she did, his arms banded tightly around her. Need prompted Alisha to move closer. She tried to think about angles and heights of chests, but she was swamped by the sensation of having the hard planes of his body fill in the gaps of her curves. His leg moved, and his groin pressed against hers. She grasped his neck, drew him in deeper. His hands traveled to her sides, flirted with the distance to her breasts. They ached, suddenly, craving his touch. Her pulse rate sped up as it did during joining, and her heart pounded. His body reacted and she felt his hardness surge against her middle. She jolted toward him. Thought fled…

David stepped away. She reached for him, to bring him back, to make him do more to her. But he grasped her hands. "Honey, we need to stop."

She opened her eyes. "What?" Desire cloaked her.

His other hand brushed her cheek again. "We, um, should stop. I think you have the hang of it."

Sanity returned in increments and she drew in a heavy breath. "Wow!" she said when she could think coherently.

He didn't answer. He just stared down at her.

"I, um, enjoyed this." She glanced down at the bulge in his pants. "You did, too."

Clearing his throat, he nodded. "I did. Any red-blooded male would react to kissing you like that, Alisha."

"I thought people of your time had to be attracted to become aroused."

"There's chemistry between the sexes."

She angled her head. "Then you aren't so different from people of my time."

Stepping even farther back, he sighed heavily. "Emotional attachment makes kissing better."

"It's better than this?"

A big laugh rumbled out of his belly.

"Are you laughing at me?"

"No. I love your frankness. Look, Lisha. Physiologically, men's and women's bodies — or the same sexes depending on gender orientation — react this way."

"Then why do you need the emotion? This was plenty good."

"Emotion itself between a man and woman is as good as physical contact."

"It can't be."

"It is. Someday, you'll see."

"Perhaps soon." He didn't respond. "Can I ask you something else?"

Briefly, he closed his eyes. "You're killin' me, Alisha."

"What do you mean?"

"Nothing. Ask away."

"I wanted you to touch my breasts, badly. Is that the purpose of kissing? To stimulate? Because it works."

"Excuse me," he said and walked out of the room, leaving her openmouthed. She heard water run from the faucet in the kitchen. She didn't know why he'd left her, so she followed him and found him staring out the window, drinking from a glass. His back faced her and she could see his wide shoulders were stiff.

"David, are you all right?"

"Yes." His voice was hoarse.

"Why did you come out here?"

He waited a beat, then pivoted. His face was taut with strain. "I needed space, to calm myself down."

"Because I aroused you."

"Yes."

"I'm sorry. I know that's painful without fulfillment."

"It'll subside."

She cocked her head. "Do you take care of your own sexual needs? We have vaginos…"

As if to block her out, he closed his eyes.

"What's wrong, David?"

"Men and women don't usually talk about those things."

"All right. I won't ask Joe the same question."

"No, I wouldn't recommend it." Now he sounded amused. "I'll answer your questions, though. Yes, I take care of my own sexual needs when I'm not dating."

She frowned. Felt a hollowness in her stomach. "That kiss made me not like the idea of you dating someone."

He laughed sardonically. "Welcome to the twenty-first century, honey."

• • •

THE FOLLOWING MORNING, David was awakened by Alisha. This time she sent a text.

*Are you up yet?*

Fuck. He'd been *up* all night. Until he had the good sense to *take care of his sexual needs by himself.*

He typed back, *Yes.*

He thought about flirting, about writing, *Why don't you join me in bed?* but he didn't. Today, he was unsure about everything. Because she'd said, *That kiss made me not like the idea of you dating someone.* The very sexy kiss caused him to be honest with himself. David had wanted to make love with her last night. He'd wanted her to be with *him,* not Joe Destino.

But he didn't know what to do about it. She was naïve, inexperienced. She was unfamiliar with emotional intimacy in today's time and how it was tied to sex. A sudden turn-around from him might confuse her. Should he hamstring her to a relationship with the first man she had physical contact with in this time? Shouldn't she have a fling, try out new things—new people? Besides, he'd given Joe the green light. Hell, David had given it to her. No, he should do the noble thing and let her get the experience she needed. If, afterward, she wanted *him,* David, then he'd go after her with a zeal usually reserved for God.

The return text read, *I'm making you breakfast. To thank you for last night.*

Though he wished she was thanking him for a lot more this morning, he texted that he'd be right over. Ten minutes later, he left through the back, crossing the grass to get to her side of the house. The table outside under the umbrella had been set. The screen door was open. It was too hot to forgo the air-conditioning, but she did that a lot. Of course, if he'd never been out in the atmosphere, he'd probably do the same. And the morning was beautiful here with geraniums the old neighbors had left in pots around the patio, the green leafy trees and some lingering yellow irises lining the side of the house.

"Good morning," he said from the entryway.

She was at the stove, her face flushed, her hair messy. "I'm bringing the food right out. Sit down out there and enjoy some coffee. It's in a decanter thing Celi bought me."

David sat and poured coffee. Like everything else she did, she made it well. Silently he said thanks to God for the beautiful day, the good coffee, for having Alisha in his life. "Let me do the right thing here," he mumbled quietly.

"Who are you talking to?" he heard behind him.

He looked up. The sunlight caught the strands of her hair, making them shiny and lighter. Her amber eyes were liquid in the morning light. "To God."

"Oh, of course. Did God talk back?"

"God always talks back. Sometimes, people just don't listen."

She sat with her cup of tea in front of her. "Still not drinking coffee?" he asked.

"No, but I am developing a taste for wine." She frowned. "Helen told me people drink the wine called champagne—we had it at The Mix—for breakfast." She shook her head. "It's hard to imagine."

Yep, she was innocent, in so many ways.

"Someday, I'll fix you a mimosa."

"That's the drink she mentioned." Her face softened. "I can't tell you how much I appreciate what you did for me last night?"

"Did for you?"

"Introducing me to sexual protocol."

"My pleasure." Literally.

"I am anxious to go on my first date."

At least he'd gotten to give her the first kiss she'd ever experience.

"I'm sure Joe is, too. I'd tell you more about him, but that's what dating is for. To get to know each other."

Her head cocked. "I knew nothing about the men I joined with in the future. I never wanted to."

"As I said before, the emotional component, brought on by getting to know each other, makes a big difference." One he was very afraid they'd already had with each other.

*Damn it, God, let us stop talking about this.*

A buzzer rang in the kitchen.

*Thank you.*

Rising, she circled around him and touched his shoulder as she passed him. It was a little thing, but he liked her unconscious gravitation toward him. She returned with a heavenly smelling dish. "What's that?"

"Strata, which means layers. The ingredients are eggs, cheese and the bacon people seem to like here."

"Guilty as charged."

After she sat, she picked up a large spoon. He stayed her hand. "May we say grace?"

Her brow furrowed. "Grace is the quality of moving fluidly. Easily."

"It's also a state of being one with God. And a prayer before meals. To show gratitude for the food, for forgiveness and the mercy of God."

"I've never seen the custom. Jess and Helen, the Lansings, they don't engage in it."

"I haven't pushed you to do it before, but now that we're spending more time together it *is* my custom."

"Go ahead. What do I do?"

"I close my eyes and let the spirit of God fill me."

Dutifully, she closed her eyes.

"Blessed Lord, we give thanks for this lovely day, this appealing food, for the relationship you've given to me and Alisha. Stay with us both throughout the day and keep us in your care. Amen."

"That was nice."

"Did you feel anything?"

"Peace."

"That's God in one form."

They ate. The food was tangy with some spice — hot sauce maybe — gooey with cheese, firm with eggs. When he finished, he said, "What a terrific meal."

"Helen's recipe. I asked her to teach me how to cook before we left for Virginia. The results are satisfactory."

"I'll give her my thanks when I see her." He rose. "I hate to eat and run, but I have to go to the hospital to visit some parishioners."

"Oh." Her tone held disappointment.

"What's wrong?"

"I was hoping you could pick among my wardrobe what I should wear tonight. Both Alisha and Dorian say I have no fashion sense." She rolled her eyes. "As if I care about that. They did purchase me some clothes for going out."

Again, David sighed heavily. If he had his way he'd dress her in a shroud. A heavy, black one. But unselfishly, he said, "I can take a few minutes to do that."

The pit in his stomach returned, and the day seemed dimmer. Fuck! Nobility sucked.

• • •

"BLESSED LORD,

I'm here on my knees, lighting this candle, so you will give me direction. Push me, sweet Jesus, to where you want me to go, what you want me to do next, *who* should be next. Each time I receive a message, I strive to do your work, fill your directive. Give me your grace and your guidance.

Your Servant always."

•  •  •

DAVID HAD JUST showered and changed into his collar and black shirt and pants to go the hospital and was trundling downstairs when the doorbell rang. *Please, don't let it be Alisha. I've had about all this date stuff I can handle right now.*

At the door, he found Jeb Morse and Brian Young, two ministers who were his friends. Tall and attractive, Jeb greeted him warmly. Smaller, more slight, Brian shook his hand and gave him what passed for smile.

"Hey, guys. Can I help you?"

Jeb put his hand on Brian's shoulder. "Brian here wanted to see you. Sorry to bother you at home."

"No bother, come on in."

They all went to the porch, which was pleasantly cool because of the two overhead fans whirring above them. "Could you get us some tea?" Jeb asked.

While he was in the kitchen, he heard the murmur of voices but couldn't make out what they were saying. When he returned, he sat and said, "Something's wrong. I can tell."

Jeb looked at Brian. Finally, Brian said, "I'm depressed. Dangerously so, Jeb thinks."

"What do *you* think?"

"I suppose I am." Brian's voice was strained. "Being without a job is tough." Both men had lost their churches to closings for lack of attendance and finances. There were more churches going defunct every day. People just weren't finding God.

"I'm sure it's hard." He spared Jeb a glance. "No luck for either of you?"

"I have a lead on an assistant pastorship." Jeb's tone was grave.

"That would be difficult. To follow, after leading so long."

"It's solid work. If I get it, I'm taking it."

"Then good for you. Brian, no options so far?"

"None."

"How are your finances? I have some money saved if you need it."

"I live frugally and have enough. I'm fine financially for a while."

"But not mentally."

"No, not mentally. I know you're a psychologist. What do you suggest I do?"

"First, you should get a complete physical to see if there's anything wrong. Then you should get counseling."

"With you?"

"It's not a good idea to counsel friends."

"I wouldn't even consider talking to anybody else."

"All right then. We can have a few chats. If I or a doctor seems to think you need more, you'll have to go to someone else."

"We'll see."

The men left and David felt bad for them. And wished like hell he could help. Sad, he went out the front door to drive to the hospital.

# CHAPTER 6

AROUND NOON, ALISHA stood in her bedroom, staring at the clothes she and David had picked out this morning. He liked the yellow dress. His eyes had sparkled when she held it up to herself, but overall he wasn't himself this morning. She'd heard visitors come to his door after he left her, then he'd gone out, too. She was rummaging around in her closet for shoes when the phone rang.

She answered on the first ring. "Alisha Law."

"Lisha, I'm glad you're there." Jess's voice came over the line, hoarse with worry.

"What's wrong?"

"I'm at the hospital. Helen got up to pee at sunrise, and she tripped on some shoes I left out and fell. She said she was okay, but the baby didn't move in an hour. We're at Memorial Hospital."

"I'll come right over."

"Can you call Dorian? I just tried Luke and can't get him."

"Yes, of course. And Celi's in New York with Madison to see some plays. I'll call her, too." She waited a beat, unsure of what to say. "Are you all right?"

"No." He choked out the word. "What if she loses this child, Alisha?"

Alisha answered firmly. "Don't think that way. It's premature." She didn't censor her words when she added, "Have a little faith."

Hands shaking after she disconnected, she sat down and pictured Helen's face when she discovered she was pregnant. Jess's grin when he touched her stomach. Their utter joy in their future, something totally unfamiliar to Alisha. Could it all be in vain? True, they'd seen chips showing her pregnancy, but that was before they changed society. No, no! She was going to do what she'd told Jess to do. Have faith. To that end, she punched in the first number to call.

"David Ryan."

Trying to control her voice, she said, "Oh, David, you have to get to Memorial Hospital. Helen's there, with some bleeding."

"I'm already here," he said calmly. "But I could come back and pick you up."

"No, I can drive there. I still have to call Dorian and Celeste. Just get to the Cromwells and offer them some hope."

"There is hope, honey, believe me. I'll go down there as soon as I'm finished with my congregant."

Comforted by his assurances, she phoned Dorian.

• • •

DAVID DIDN'T GET to see Helen until twenty minutes after Alisha's call. His congregant was going into surgery and he had to pray with him, then reassure the family. All the while, Helen was in the back of his mind. The Cromwells didn't deserve this kind of tragedy, if indeed the miscarriage happened; they'd already been through so much.

When he strode into the waiting area, he located Alisha right away, sitting on one of the vinyl chairs. Funny, he'd never once seen her vulnerable...fragile, even when Luke got shot and everyone was on edge. But now, she seemed as if a stiff wind could blow her over. He smiled, wondering what she'd think of the idiom.

When he reached her, he said softly, "Alisha?"

She looked up with eyes full of concern. "David. I'm glad you're here. Dorian and Luke and Celi haven't arrived yet."

Sitting down next to her, he took her hand. He knew she wasn't comfortable with public displays of affection, but he did it anyway. Her skin was ice cold.

"Any news?"

"Some. I got to go into the room before the doctor saw Helen, and I scanned her with the Multimed. But it wasn't a lot of help. The thing went haywire." She gave him a sardonic smile. "It's never encountered fetuses."

"Did it give any information?"

"On its screen, I could see the heartbeat."

"That should be good news."

"Jess didn't think so, because the child still hasn't moved." She squeezed his fingers. "I even put my hand on her stomach to nudge it, and nothing happened."

"Then we'll pray until we hear."

"Pray? Talk to your god? You earnestly don't think your god has any control over this, do you? It's a physiological issue."

"As a matter of fact, I wouldn't ask God to make Helen all right. Come on, I'll show you." At her hesitance, he said, "You liked saying grace this morning."

"I guess."

"Bow your head." He still held one of her hands and took the other. "Precious Lord, please be here in our midst during this uncertain time. Help Jess and Helen to cope with the anxiety of waiting, with the knowledge that something could happen to Baby Jessica. Be with Helen and Jess as they face the unknown. Amen."

When he raised his eyes, she looked at him. "That was as nice as grace."

"Did it make you feel better?"

"No, what I meant was, that you put Jess and Helen's needs above ours. I have to say, it was comforting."

He winked at her. "I was going to ask my God to watch over you, too, be with you as you forge a new life. But I was afraid you'd get mad."

"No, no, I wouldn't get mad. Only puzzled."

"David? Alisha?" The question came from Luke, who now stood before them. His clothes and hair were rumpled, but the expression in his eyes made David take in a breath. Dorian clung to him, white-faced. A foot or so back, Celeste hovered.

Reaching out, David grasped Luke's shoulder. "We know a little more than Jess said in the phone call." He focused on Alisha.

She said, "I ran the Multimed over Helen's stomach. It showed the heartbeat. I looked it up. That means the child is alive."

Dorian dropped down next to Alisha. "I hope so."

They both glanced simultaneously at Celeste. David tracked their gazes. Celi had her hand on her stomach, was staring down at it. Alisha said, "Celi, come over here."

When she didn't move, Alisha stood and crossed to her. She grasped Celi's shoulders much as David had done to Luke. "Just because Helen may have had some bleeding, doesn't mean you will."

Dorian had followed her and sidled up to Celeste. "Celi, what she says is true."

The bleakest eyes raised to them. David has seen similar looks in congregants when they'd lost a loved one, and soldiers whose buddies were killed in war. "Is it? True? If it could happen…" She trailed off, and her gaze landed on Luke, who was staring at her. "Why, yes, of course, we're both going to be all right."

Luke jammed his hands in his pockets and moved closer to David. "I don't think Helen or Celeste can handle a miscarriage." He spoke softly, his eyes misting. "Or Jess."

"As I told Alisha, don't buy trouble."

Ten minutes later, Jess came out from the ER. David was swamped by relief when he saw Jess's face—haggard but unlined. Almost smiling.

"Good news. The baby's fine. That *was* the fetal heartbeat on the multi thing, but more so, the doctor did an ultrasound, and everything seems to be as it should. No puncture of the placenta, no ruptures."

"Hallelujah." This from Luke.

David glanced over at the women again. They'd leaned into each other. Since future women were unable to bear children, he was aware of how much Helen's pregnancy had affected them. Luke, too, took Jess in a big bear hug.

Raising his eyes to the heavens, he smiled. "Thanks, God."

He swore he heard a *You're welcome.*

•  •  •

THE FIZZ, AS they said in this time, had gone out of Alisha. As she opened her front door, all she wanted to do was collapse. Behind her, David asked, "Are you going to be all right?"

She pivoted. The features of his face relaxed into an easy smile. She loved that about him, that he could always see the good in everything; he instilled hope in all of them, and of course, in a crisis, he was a boulder. No, no, a rock. "Yes. Thank you for your help today. I was…uplifted by you."

"What a nice thing to say." Raising his hand, he ran a knuckle under one eye. "You've got smudges here." He glanced at his watch. "You have a few hours before Joe picks you up." There was that furrowed brow and stiffened shoulders again. "Why don't you take a nap?"

"I've never slept during the day in my life, but I might. The emotion in that waiting room exhausted me. With her sensitivity, Celi must be hurting."

"I suppose." He cocked his head. "Sometimes, it isn't good to feel too much."

The statement was ominous.

"Is something wrong, David?"

"No of course not. Helen's fine. Everybody is. I just have a lot on my mind."

"All right, then. Will you see Joe before he comes here?"

"Probably." This time he chucked her under the chin. "Remember what I taught you."

"As if I could forget."

Still tense, he turned, walked out. Closing the door behind him, she leaned against it with the odd urge to call him back, ask him to lie with her to rest. And maybe do more. She shook her head. She must be really tired.

In her bedroom, the three-in-the-afternoon sun peaked through the slats in the blinds. She closed them tighter and began to disrobe. The benefit of living alone was she could sleep naked now, as she always had, as all people of her time had. After shedding her clothes, she left them on the floor and climbed between the sheets. Heat filtered in through the open windows, so she didn't use the covers. Closing her eyes, she dozed.

*As she came down the stairs, he stood by the doorway, dressed in a black-and-white checked shirt, black pants and a big grin on his face. "You're not ready," he said hoarsely, taking in her naked body.*

*"That depends on what you have in mind."*

*"A date – movie and dinner."*

*She gave him a sexy look. "Okay. I'll just go back up and dress."*

*She'd climbed two steps when she felt him snag her waist from behind. He pulled her against him. "Not so fast." He bit her neck. "Witch."*

*Alisha chuckled. It was unbelievably sexy with him standing behind her on the stairs – they only joined in sleeping chambers in the future – his clothes abrading her skin. His scent, woodsy, so male, seemed to transfer to her pores. He whispered, "Let*

*me make you come. Right here."*

*"All right, David, you can make me come. Then I'll return the favor…"*

Alisha awakened herself with a loud moan. And with a final jerk of her body. Her skin was slick with sweat and she was panting. She'd been dreaming and climaxed in real time. It had happened before, of course, but not since she'd arrived in the twenty-first century.

She closed her eyes to recreate the memory. Then she remembered. It hadn't been Joe Destino behind her on the stairs. It had been David.

"Megadamn," she said out loud. "Mega*damn.*"

Why would she dream about the man, the reverend? "Okay," she spoke again. "I'm attracted to him." That didn't come as a shock, but the feelings discomfited her. She didn't want to be attracted to a minister. A man who believed in a god he would love more than her.

Not that she wanted to be loved by a man.

Did she? Dorian and Celeste were so happy.

"Arrgh!" She bounded out of bed, slipped on the robe, went to the window to let in the light.

And there he was. In a far corner of the backyard, he'd planted a ten-by-ten square vegetable garden. Alisha was mesmerized when he told her the seeds would sprout and become lettuce, tomatoes, cucumbers and a variety of other vegetables. Still to come were potatoes and carrots and a thing called a pumpkin.

Right now, though, she wasn't thinking about the sustenance. Instead, she was mesmerized by the play of his muscles along his back, how his arms strained with the weeding. If she was closer, would she see him sweating, smell the scent of hard work and man?

Her still-tender genital parts stirred. Oh, hellor.

• • •

THANKS FOR LETTING *this be so hard*, David told God sarcastically as he yanked the stubborn weeds from a section of the treed lot. He'd finished the garden, but he wasn't ready to face Alisha and craved more physical exertion. He should have left the house so he wouldn't have to see her in the pretty yellow dress they'd chosen—that he'd helped her choose—but somehow he couldn't. "Fuck!"

"Swearin' at the weeds?" Joe Destino's voice came from behind him, and David took a deep breath.

*Let me be nice.*

Falling back on his knees, he glanced over his shoulder. Joe was carrying a bouquet of wildflowers. His eyes narrowed. "Hey, you okay?"

David stood. "Yeah, nice flowers. She'll like them." He hadn't realized he knew things about her: she brought buds into her house every day, she preferred chicken over steak, breezy nights, white wine when she indulged, and she was fascinated by kittens. Maybe he'd get her one.

"David?"

"Sorry, it's been a long day." He described what had happened with Helen. "But I think Alisha took a nap, so she should be good to go."

Joe gave a very male laugh. "Since you told me to be careful with her, I won't take that the wrong way. Or maybe the right way."

David forced a smile. Past Joe, he saw the sliding doors to her half of the house open and Alisha step out. Yep, the yellow sundress looked good on her. The cloth kissed her shoulders and breasts. Clung to her hips. *Stop that line of thinking,* he told himself. The dress would be perfect for the hot weather, but he hoped she remembered to take the sweater that matched it for air-conditioning. "There she is."

Joe turned.

Alisha's gait was a little different as she walked toward them. Her shoes had a bit of a heel and made her hips sway. Shit.

"Hi, Joe. David." She nodded to the flowers. "Are those for me?"

Joe was the first man to bring her a bouquet.

"Of course. You look great, Alisha."

"Thanks." She inhaled the gardenias. "Oh, wow."

Joe cocked his head. "You like?"

"I like."

"Ready for dinner?"

"Yes."

When she focused on David, he noticed her cheeks flushed. Why?

"David, are you going to work all night?" She sounded concerned.

"No, just till sundown."

Joe socked him on the arm. "No date?"

"Nope. But I have a group thing tonight at church."

"Do you attend church, Joe?" Alisha asked.

"Afraid not."

"Maybe we can discuss why. I don't, either."

"Sure, doll. We can do anything we want."

Her eyes narrowed at the use of *doll*.

"Watch out calling her a plaything. She's a staunch feminist."

Joe grasped her elbow. "I'm dying to find out all sorts of things about her."

"Then you should go."

"I left my sweater inside. I'll just go get it. And put the flowers in a vase."

"I'll come with you," Joe remarked.

Both shot him a quick glance. "Good-bye, David."

"Have fun you kids," he said lightly.

"Yes, Dad," Joe mocked.

David watched them head into the house.

His heart clenched in his chest. Incredibly sad, he turned back to the weeds.

• • •

IN A ROOM filled with the musicals of a piano, tables with white cloths and plush chairs, Alisha said to the serving person, "I'd like the broiled chicken and broccoli. Iced water to drink."

The young man smiled. "Want to try our famous Swiss cheese sauce on the chicken?"

"No, thank you. Cheese contains five grams of saturated fat and seven-point-eight grams total per ounce. Though the calcium is good for human bone density."

He stared at her oddly. She didn't know why. "Okay." He turned to Joe. "You, sir?"

"I'll have the twenty-four-ounce prime rib. Baked potato, loaded. An order of onion rings." He winked at Alisha. "I'm not watching my waistline."

"You…" Wait a minute. That must be an idiom. Ah, to want to be slender.

"I'm not, either. But I limit my intake of fat."

"We'll have the chocolate lava cake for dessert," Joe added. To her he said, "It takes a while to prepare."

That irked Alisha. She didn't eat sweets, either. Celeste loved them, but she avoided them.

When the waiter left, Joe picked up the bottle of cabernet he'd ordered and poured her some. "That's enough," she said as sweetly as she could.

He filled her glass to the top, then did the same with his. "David said you don't go out much. That you grew up in South America. Is that why you're so picky about your food?"

David had talked to him about her? She had a vivid image of her with David on the stairs, his hand sliding around her, to touch her intimately. *It was a dream. Remember that.*

"Am I? Picky? I prefer to think of it as being circumspect."

"Tell me more about how you grew up."

The story had become etched in her brain. Mother and Father, missionaries. Spoke English as a second language…

"I see. Did you like being so sheltered?"

"I knew nothing different. Until I came to the United States for college."

He sipped more of the ruby red liquid. "What did you major in?"

Major? "I, um, studied anthropology. It's fascinating. What about you?"

"No college." He picked up a slice of bread, put fat on it, then bit off a section. "I went into the service after high school."

"You were stationed in the Armed Services with David?"

"Yes, he came in older than I did."

"Is that what you meant by calling him Dad?" Something that made him frown.

"No, I was teasing him about watching over you."

She didn't know what to say to that, so she took a sip of her wine. It tasted smooth, though she liked white better.

"David was a Godsend over there, pardon the pun. Guys went to him with deep-seated guilt. His job was to console them, advise them." Joe shook his head. "Since he was also a psychologist, he had the power to keep them out of combat."

*Choices had to be made. Difficult ones. I still dream about some of mine that went bad.*

"That must have been difficult for him."

Joe nodded and got a faraway look in his eyes. "There was this one time he'd told the captain he thought one of the privates was ready to go back outside the wire."

Out of the safe zone. She knew because David had explained the term.

"What happened?"

"The whole platoon was killed. David was beside himself."

"Upset?"

"Yes. I thought he was going to leave the camp, but he didn't. I'm afraid more of those kinds of things happened to him."

"Poor David."

Joe changed the subject after that, and Alisha was glad to end talk about David. She kept thinking about him tonight. How he'd yanked the weeds from the garden with brute force. How his skin had been covered with sweat, as she'd imagined from her window. His arms had been dirty, grit clinging to them.

"Why is it that you don't go to church, Joe?"

He shook his head. "I see too much death to believe in a supreme being."

David had seen it, too. But he took the opposite route.

When the chocolate lava cake arrived, Joe insisted she have a couple of bites. It was sweet and smelled wonderful, but she didn't want to be sick. For some reason, her stomach was queasy.

"So, do you still want to see the movie? Or we could drive out to the lake. There's a summer fair this week. Firefighters have had calls to it."

"Is the view of the lake visible?" She still hadn't gone to the beach, seen the real bodies of water in this time period. There had been too much to do.

"Yep. The spot is right on the lake. You'd like the games and rides. My favorite is the Ferris wheel."

What the hellor was that? She hadn't encountered the term in her research. She just nodded.

"Then, the lake it is."

They drove listening to musicals (they had no songs or instruments in the future) coming out of the radio box. Alisha was glad not to have to talk. Making conversation where she had to be on guard not to reveal her secrets was exhausting.

The area where the fair was held pulsed with lights and a cacophony of sounds. For a moment, the noise and glare shocked her senses. As they approached the grounds, her stomach churned. She told herself this was a new experience and to enjoy it, but the bombardment of so many sights, sounds and smells was clearly giving her sensory overload.

Joe stopped at a booth. "This is my favorite. Shall I win you a bear?"

She swallowed hard, knowing she was missing the meaning. "What would I do with it?"

"Put it on your bed." He leaned over and kissed her nose. "And think of me when you see the hairy little fellow."

Confused, Alisha examined the game. Ah, the bears were inanimate objects. Bright pinks and blues. Round, black eyes. They made her smile.

Bear in hand, Joe stopped for cotton candy next, the strong scent offensive. He tore off a piece and held it to her mouth. A man would feed you on a date? She stepped back. "No, thank you."

After a few more visits to games, they came upon the rides.

"This is the Ferris wheel."

Alisha looked up and gawked. "Oh, by the godheads, it's huge."

"You've never seen one?" Suspicion worked its way into his tone.

"Um, no. As I said, I grew up isolated, and there was no time for these kinds of activities when I became an adult." That at least was true. She'd been busy trying to save the world.

"There had to have been fairs in South America."

"Not that I attended." She eyed the ride with caution. "The mechanism doesn't look safe."

"It is. I've been on them tons of times."

Again, she stepped back. "I prefer not to. I'll watch you."

"Come on, Alisha," he said, tugging on her arm. "Loosen up."

That must mean she was being too reticent. Still…

"I don't think so."

He moved in close and put his arm around her. His scent was very male, appealing, but she didn't experience any feeling of…the need to join. "Please."

Reluctantly, she agreed. They waited at the bottom of the ride for the next compartment to stop. When it did, the two of them climbed into the five-by-three box. Joe sat close, his body aligning with hers. Reaching his arm over her — it brushed her breasts and she felt no response — he snapped the belt. Then he slid his other arm fully around her shoulders. "There. This is great."

She didn't answer, but the night air drifted off the lake and the breeze soothed her. She was sweating from the heat.

Apparently, each time a new person boarded the ride, all the cars stopped. The action made her stomach pitch and she breathed deeply.

"Scared?" he asked.

*Not when your society has survived cyber wars.*

"No. I don't like stopping and starting."

"That part will be over soon."

It was and the ride began in earnest. When they moved with no stops, she felt better.

"Look at the stars from here." He pointed upward as they circled the top.

The stars were closer and that was fun, but as on the descent, the car jerked and swayed, and she felt her stomach heave. *Oh, Nord, please. Let this stop.*

She tried to turn away, but he yanked her closer.

It was the wrong move to make.

• • •

WHEN DAVID PULLED up to the church, he saw his kids under the makeshift lights they'd installed to shine on the basketball court. Exhausted, and worried about Alisha, David nonetheless couldn't let these guys down. They needed him. They weren't gang kids, just troublemakers at school and ignored by parents. David took pleasure in the fact that they wanted to be with him occasionally, wanted an adult to look up to. And they talked about their lives.

"There he is," one boy, Mince, called out. "About time."

"Hey, punk. I got other things to do, you know." He smiled to take the edge off his words. They expected some attitude from him, and tonight, David felt full of it.

The five boys stood around in a semicircle, and David went up to each of them, gave them a variety of handshakes, then they set out to play. Three against three. David prayed for physical strength. His team did pretty well, though the other won.

The boys hadn't come here tonight for basketball, anyway. As a group, they headed to the kitchen in the fellowship hall. "What kind you got?" Jase asked, taking a seat at the big island in the kitchen. The others followed suit.

"Vanilla, chocolate and butterscotch sauce, sprinkles."

"What kinda sprinkles?" Buzz, their leader, asked.

When David finished serving the ice cream—the boys would clean up—he sat with a big bowl of chocolate and waited for them to begin talking. The treat was cool and sweet, and he savored it. Savored these kids. And tried not to think of a certain date that was going on right now.

"Yo, Rev. I got a question." Louie, a small Puerto Rican boy who had been abused by his uncle spoke up. "How come girls are so stupid?"

"Explain what you mean."

"This *chica*, she acts like she digs me, but when I get close, she pushes me away."

He didn't particularly want to answer queries about women. What the hell did he know about them, anyway?

"Maybe it's because you got a small dick," Cork remarked.

"She ain't seen it yet, smartass. Why, Rev?"

"Maybe she's shy. Some girls seem in control and cool about everything, but they're really shy."

Which made him think about Alisha. She *was* shy, and he hoped Destino was abiding by his promise to behave with her.

Buzz had an issue with a teacher. "I hate her. I get Cs, and she keeps pushing me to do better. Why?"

"Probably because she sees what I see in you."

"What's that? A dope?" Mince teased.

"No, a very smart guy who could, if he wanted to, go to college." Buzz knew his way around a computer like no kid David had ever seen. Almost as good as Alisha.

They booed at David's comment, but he'd made his point.

By ten, they'd all gotten what they needed from him, except Jase, a rich kid who had mega problems with his family. David suspected he was gay, and that was the root of a lot of his turmoil. "Hey, Jase, you want to stay back a minute?"

"Nah, I'm runnin' with the hooligans tonight."

Hooligans? Why did the boy's use of that word bother him? "Be safe, you guys."

Dead on his feet, he drove home, made it upstairs, collapsed on the bed. And woke, startled, at midnight. Damn it all. He was still tired. Knowing he wouldn't go back to sleep, he got up. He was sitting at his desk waiting for Alisha to come home, wondering where she was, if they were having a good time, if Joe touched her. When Joe's car pulled up,

David leaned back in the chair and watched them come up the walk. He was in the dark, but they were illuminated by the outdoor lamppost he'd turned on. They weren't bumping hips. Joe wasn't even holding her hand. What was he, made of stone?

They reached the door, and David saw Alisha extend her hand. Joe shook and mumbled something, then trundled down the walkway.

David didn't hear her go inside, and the car pulled away. Then a knock came on *his* door. Slowly, he got up and went to answer it. She stood on his stoop, and in the glow from her front light, he could see she was pale. And her hands trembled some. "Dear God in heaven, if he tried something with you that you didn't want, I'll beat him to a pulp."

"What?" A frown. "Oh, no, he didn't."

"You're pale and trembling. What happened?"

She said simply, "You should have warned me about Ferris wheels."

"What do you mean?"

"The ride. Joe talked me into going on one. I, um, I think the term you use is barf. I barfed all over him."

David burst out laughing.

She didn't think it was funny, he could tell.

Trying to inject sobriety and sympathy into his response, he reached for her hand. "Aw, you poor thing. Come on inside. I'll get a compress for your head and give you some seltzer."

"Anything to make me feel better."

He led her to his wide leather couch. Pushed her shoulders to sit down. "Stay upright until I get the medicine."

When he returned, she was very still. He handed her the glass filled with fizzy liquid.

"Drink this."

She sipped and wrinkled her nose. "It tastes bad."

"It'll help." When she'd consumed the whole thing, he said, "Lie down."

Like a child — a youngling — she did as he ordered. She shivered when her skin met the cold leather. Reaching for a throw, he covered her, then put the compress on her face.

"That's soothing."

"I'm sorry I didn't tell you about amusement parks."

She sighed. "It wasn't just that. He kept pouring me wine. And he ordered a chocolate thing and insisted I have three bites."

"That many?" He tried to keep the humor from his voice.

"Are you laughing at me?"

"No, honest to God." He was laughing because the date he'd been worrying about all night had gone south. Joyfully, *very* south.

She placed her hand on her stomach and closed her eyes. "I wish my internal organs would heal."

"You can't use the Multimed on an upset stomach?"

"We never have this kind of illness. And it's mostly for sprains or bruises, even wounds. It won't help me."

"Then I will." He brushed his knuckles down her cheek. "Rest. You'll be fine in a while."

"I'm very tired. We engaged in tedious conversations. He isn't as easy to talk to as you are."

"Probably because you don't have to cover up as much with me. Who you are. What you don't understand."

"I thought the same thing." She touched his arm. "David, I wasn't as interested in him as I am in you."

"Why, thank you."

He got up once to refresh the cloth. When he returned, he saw her shiver again. "Shall I turn off the air? I know you don't use it consistently."

She watched him, her brow furrowed. "No, I like it too hot for you." Again she closed her eyes. "But I don't want to leave your home yet."

"You don't have to leave at all."

Her eyes were huge in her face when she opened them. "Do you, um, David, could you lay down next me to for a while? Your body generates heat—"

He wanted to roll his eyes at that one.

"—and I'm feeling vulnerable right now."

Huh! Wasn't this something? Alisha had been instrumental in perfecting time travel, come here at great cost and helped two people change the world. She'd also faced down a criminal trying to hurt Jess. But tonight, her body had betrayed her and she needed his comfort. "Sure."

They maneuvered until he stretched out beside her. Slid his arm under her neck. As if she'd been doing this forever, she turned into him and nestled right in the crook of his arm and shoulder. "This feels good."

She had that one right.

They stayed on his couch until her eyes closed and David's lids began to droop.

A loud ringing. David shifted and something nudged into him. More ringing, then, a voice.

He came awake slowly to find Alisha wrapped around him.

Before he could react, he heard, "It's Kerry. David, pick up. There's been another fire."

# CHAPTER 7

THE FIRST UNIVERSALIST Church on Morrison Avenue wasn't burned to the ground, which was what Alisha had expected before she and David pulled up to the scene. "I don't see any damage."

"Me, either. Maybe the fire started in the back. The fire trucks are here." He pointed to the huge red-and-white vehicles, which emitted a scent so strong it permeated through the closed windows. She also noted the small white Jeep that read, Fire Investigator. She wondered if Joe Destino was the one in charge.

"I'm going with you," she said as he opened the door of the car.

"God, I never realized how many fumes the trucks gave off." He looked at her. "Your stomach okay?"

"Don't worry about me. Let's see what happened." He'd told her on the way over that Hal Hanson, the minister of this church, was a close friend of his and when he phoned Kerry back, she said Hal had been hurt. He had no more details than that.

They hurried to the rear of the building. Oh, no. The attachment to the church was smoldering, and Alisha could smell the burned wood and hear the sizzling as the fire department doused the structure with water.

David said, "There's Hal."

Tracking his gaze, she caught sight of Hal with a blanket around his shoulders, sitting on the edge of a truck marked Medical. A uniformed man stood next to him. As they got closer, she saw that burns raised angry welts on his arms and hands. Alisha stayed back and let David approach him alone.

David settled a hand on his friend's shoulder. "Hal, are you all right?"

Hal looked up. His eyes were squinted, and there were smudges on his face. "Yeah. Got some burns, though."

Alisha studied him. She could tell the burns were second degree. The Multimed could heal them easily. David glanced at the paramedic. "How bad is it?"

Her name tag read Thomas. "Second degree. We can treat them right here."

David took a seat next to Hal. "What happened?"

"I stumbled across him."

"Who?"

"The arsonist. He'd torched the fellowship hall already. When he saw me, he took off."

"How'd you get burned?"

"I ran in the side door and got the fire extinguisher." He shook his head. "I know; it was foolish. But the hall is brand new, and my congregation worked so hard to raise money to build it."

"We can rebuild."

"Of course."

David slid his arm around Hal's shoulders. "But it's hard."

"I called nine-one-one. Thank God the flames didn't reach the church."

God had nothing to do with the situation! Hal's explanation angered Alisha. These were two men who spent their entire lives bringing their god to others, and this was how the supposed supreme being repaid them? She was glad she didn't believe.

A firefighter approached in bulky yellow pants and coat. It was indeed Joe. "Hey, David." He nodded to her. "Alisha."

"Did you find the same evidence as in the other two fires?" David asked him.

"Yes. And the reverend gave us a description of his height, weight, etcetera. He's male, but he wore a mask." Joe said to Hal, "Your observations are a great help."

Before Joe turned away, he approached Alisha and tugged her to the side. "Hey, I'm sorry last night turned out so badly."

"So am I. I'll pay to have your clothes cleaned."

"No need." He frowned. "You got the same dress on still."

Uh-oh. "I, um, was sick again and went next door to see if David had medication. I slept on his couch" — with David, which had been heaven — "because he was worried about me. We came right over when the phone woke us."

"Us?"

"David heard it, too."

Another firefighter called Joe away, and Alisha breathed more easily. She hadn't expected to answer questions about last night. David had held her, shared his body heat and cuddled her close all night long. Never had she experienced such a sense of well-being and safety. In the future, people didn't actually sleep with each other, so she'd had no idea how nice that would be.

They waited until midmorning while Hal talked to the police and Joe again. David did not leave Hal's side, and Alisha separated herself from him so she didn't get in the way. Alone, she sat on a bench, staring at the big stone structure behind the burned ruins. She was feeling so negative about his god, she hoped he didn't ask her about it.

ion KATHRYN SHAY

Finally, the site was contained. She was affected by Hal, who stood in the deserted yard now, his shoulders hunched, talking softly to David. Finally, they approached her. "We're going to take Hal home." David's voice was hoarse.

Reaching out, she squeezed Hal's arm, the part that wasn't covered in gauze. "I'm so sorry, Reverend Hanson."

"Me, too. At least we have more information on the arsonist."

"That's good."

Sitting in the backseat of the car, she listened to David work his own brand of miracles. His tone was soothing, his message—no one was hurt badly, we'll rebuild, God will help us through it—seemed to comfort Hal. Not Alisha, though. No way.

When they reached his home, she waited in the car while David got his friend settled inside. A group of people showed up and went into the house. David eventually came out. She'd climbed in the front seat, and he slid into the driver's side. "Those were his deacons. They came to sit with him and pray."

As he started the car, she was silent, not wanting to burden him with her angry thoughts.

"Damn it. Something has to happen before—" He stopped and raised his eyes to the heavens. "Sorry, I know You're here."

Again the silence as they drove.

He glanced at her. "You don't believe that, do you?"

"David, now's not the time to talk about theology. You're upset because of your friend."

Swerving the car into a parking section of something called a 7-Eleven, he stopped the vehicle and turned off the engine. "I want to know what you're thinking."

"All right. If your god really exists, it would have prevented the fire. Hellor, it would have prevented the ills of the future."

90

He shook his head. "That's the age-old complaint about God, and it's not valid."

"How exactly?"

"God doesn't bring about the evil in the world."

"Then who does?"

"Mankind."

"Why doesn't god keep mankind from doing bad things?"

"Because we have free will."

"Why do we have free will?"

"I don't know. It's just how we evolved."

"Didn't god create us, in your view? I read that in some tomes I've perused."

"I think God created this lovely earth. God infused it with life and we developed from that life." He gave a grim smile. "And before you ask, no I don't buy the Adam and Eve story."

"You don't believe in your Bible?"

"I do, but not like you mean. The Bible is the work of men who were interpreting God's mission on earth. We made a mistake centuries ago believing it's to be taken literally."

Alisha thought that through. "Then, what do you believe is god's role in your lives?"

"I told you this before. God is here to help us make our way through life—the good and the bad things. To celebrate our joys. To cry with us when sadness overcomes us. To give us courage and grace. To love us."

"That makes more sense."

"But you don't believe it?"

"I'm sorry, David, no."

He sighed. And she felt bad. "Let's end this conversation. It's upsetting you."

"Maybe."

"What would make you feel better?"

"You know what? I'd like to go for a bike ride. Clear my head. Get some exercise. Will you come with me?"

"Yes, of course. I'd do anything to make you feel better right now."

She was surprised to find that notion didn't scare her at all.

• • •

"I'M SO SORRY, Blessed Lord. I failed. You wanted more from me and I let you down. I'll punish myself if you will forgive me. I'll do better. Next time, there will be death. I know you want that as a sign. Perhaps I'll go back to this church and make things right. No, no, I won't cry. I won't let these tears shed. I'm doing your work, though I did it badly today. But I'll be better. I promise.

Your Servant always."

• • •

POTS AND PANS banged, a fan whirred and the low murmur of workers in the Salem Soup Kitchen pervaded the large basement space. The scent of food—it smelled like beef—also filled the air. With David by her side—Alisha was getting used to that-they descended the steps, and he was greeted warmly.

He said to her, "I hope this isn't too much for you."

He looked cute today wearing a pair of jeans (tight) and a red-collared shirt.

"I'm completely recovered from my bout of nausea the other night." She moved in closer and whispered, "If I can travel through time, I think I can serve some food."

David had suggested she accompany him to this place, where he volunteered weekly and where several of his parishioners also donated time. She had the feeling he was luring her into his congregation by including her in activities.

He grasped Alisha's elbow and led her into the crowd. "There's someone I want you to meet."

Pat, the volunteer coordinator, welcomed her warmly. A kind-looking woman with a white paper hat on her head, she smiled. "Thanks for coming. Who would you like to assist today?"

"David?"

"I don't serve food," he told her. "I sit and talk to the guests. How about Ann over there?" He pointed to another worker.

David introduced them, Ann explained to her how to serve the sixteen people they were assigned, then an older woman banged a metal spoon against a metal counter and called out, "Quiet please."

The fans were turned off and conversation ceased. Announcements were made and David began to pray. Here was religion again, entrenched in people's lives. She wondered briefly how the homeless and hungry outside the kitchen doors felt about the concept of god.

When they wheeled their carts out to the floor, the first thing Alisha noted was the sour smell of body odor and something else. "What is that smell, Ann? I know some of it is from unwashed bodies but there's something else."

"Alcohol." Ann frowned. "Most of the people who come here are addicted."

Another tragedy of this time period. People abused chemical substances. When her society righted itself, drugs and alcohol were no longer a part of it. They barely needed medicine since everyone kept fit and healthy and they had the Multimed.

Ann greeted the groups warmly, and she and Alisha served bread, fat and milk. "Thank the Lord for you," one of the guests said to Alisha.

Alisha gave a wan smile.

Next they picked up the food—a slab of beef on bread—called a hamburger, though it contained no pork—and green beans. While the guests ate the main meal, she and Ann fetched dessert. "We have time for a breather now," Ann told her after the sweets were served, as they walked to the side of the large room. Ann nodded to the group. "David is such a doll."

Doll? "Yes, he is a nice man." Who at that moment was sitting with a family of five and feeding a child while the adults ate lunch. "What will he discuss with them?"

"Maybe their situation to see if he can help. Maybe God, if they bring Him up."

"You think god is male?"

Ann thought for a moment. "No, not really. Just habit, calling God him."

"Patriarchal societies have believed that for centuries."

"I guess. Truthfully, I don't think it matters. People see God in their images."

She noted the variety of colors of people's skin. There were different races in her time, too, but society had combined so many gene pools by then, the demarcations weren't as great. "So that family believes in a black god."

"Probably."

That discussion gave her something to think about. Ann was called away, and Alisha watched as David went from table to table. Smiles wreathed the faces of those he sat with. He put his arm around a man or a woman who looked particularly sad, and something about the gesture squeezed Alisha's heart. His goodness often overwhelmed her.

She needed to give her feelings for David some thought. He had become important to her, in many ways, particularly since she admitted she was attracted to him. But she didn't want or need a relationship with a male. She *did* crave someone to join with, though. Briefly, she wondered if he'd be interested in only sex. The dream she had about him the other day had stayed with her, even now, in the midst of helping this society's unfortunate denizens.

• • •

DAVID KNEW HE was in too deep when he sat across from Alisha at the Cromwells' dining table and savored her presence. Savored the others, too. He'd always been close to Jess and Helen, and liked Luke, so getting to know Dorian and Alisha was a bonus. It had been nearly five months since he met them, but already he was used to the Sisters of Doom in his life. Especially Alisha.

And he wanted her in bed. Badly.

"I'm famished," he remarked after he said grace. His carnal thoughts were accepted by God, who wouldn't be mad he had them so close to prayers.

"Why wouldn't you be hungry? I can't believe you bicycled over here." Helen with the rounded belly made the statement.

"Alisha insisted." He winked at her. "She keeps me active. I swear I've lost ten pounds since she moved next to me."

Alisha gave him a female perusal. And it hit him then— she was silently flirting, assessing his body.

"Alisha, I saved you some plain macaroni." Helen passed her a bowl.

"I think you should try some of the marinara sauce." Dorian plucked a dumpling from her plate and put it in her mouth. "These gnocchi are wonderful."

"I'm having meat," Alisha told her. "That has sauce. It is good, Helen. But I'm still not used to so much food."

He caught her gaze. She smiled, remembering the night they spent on the couch. Was he remembering when real food had caused her to seek him out?

Dinner progressed with much laughter and discussion of everyday events. Then things turned sober. David talked about the last fire and how his friend Hal had been hurt. Luke questioned him on that, asking if they'd gotten any more leads. Unfortunately, the answer was no. And it saddened him. He'd been needing to ask Alisha and Dorian something for a while now, but he hesitated because he didn't want to abuse their friendship or get into too much serious discussion this lovely Sunday afternoon.

Then when Dorian said, "I wish there was something Luke and I could do to help," he considered that a sign.

So after they finished eating, he cleared his throat. "I'd like to ask you and Alisha something."

"Of course," Dorian responded.

"Your computellers? They have a record of our time period on them, right?"

"Yes." From Dorian. "You were present on numerous occasions when we gave you a look at the future."

"We have no idea if the records are accurate now, though." This from Alisha.

"Because we changed the future." Dorian stated it as fact.

"Yes. What's on the chips is a record previous to our actions. A new set of history chips probably exists."

Damn. David had wanted to hear something different.

"Why, David?" Jess queried.

"I was hoping we could use the chips to find out who's setting the fires. But if they might not be correct…"

Dorian suggested, "It wouldn't hurt to try."

"Yes, it would."

All eyes focused on Alisha.

"What do you mean, Lisha?"

"I've been pondering whether or not to collect the computellers from Dorian and Celeste for safekeeping."

"From what?" Luke asked.

"Now that we've hopefully changed the future, I don't think it's wise to risk other alterations we might accidentally make if we use the computellers to change your time period."

David hadn't thought about that.

"Maybe not." Luke faced her with challenge in his eyes. "If there's some information on there about the arsonist, it could just give the investigators a lead to pursue."

"And if they learn who the arsonist is because we told them, they wouldn't have known that the first time through, so to speak, so we'd be altering history again."

"That's a bit dramatic, isn't it?" Luke was needling Alisha, as he frequently did.

"No more dramatic than saving your brother's life."

He lifted his beer glass to her. "Touché."

"Luke, this isn't a contest between you and me. We're on the same side. We completed our tasks and changed the future. We can't modify society any more without risking negative repercussions." She shook her head. "I'm sorry, but I have to insist on this. Our interference must stop with Alex, with our last task, assigned by the Guardians."

Reaching for her hand, he squeezed it. "I understand." And he did. "I shouldn't have asked."

"It was all right to ask. *I* wish we could help you."

"No worries."

But the notion plagued him the rest of the afternoon. It must have shown, because Alisha got him alone outside on the patio before they left. "I can tell you're sad."

"I'm trying to shake it. I do understand."

"Maybe we can use the computeller to calculate possibilities from only the information we have in this time. That's how I employed it, updating the computers at church."

"That would be interfering, wouldn't it?"

"It seems different, but maybe not."

Giving her a pretend smile, he said, "I have confidence in our legal system. They'll find the guy. I just hope it's before anyone is killed."

About four in the afternoon, they rode their bikes home while the day was still warm. When the sidewalk narrowed, David appreciated watching Alisha's body ahead of him and let himself fantasize for a bit.

A sudden jolt. Metal. The bike hurtled forward, then he catapulted over the handle bars. He tasted dirt and grass as his face hit the lawn.

"By the godheads!"

A screech of tires.

And all of David's body began to ache.

• • •

TRYING TO ERASE the memory of David lying on the ground, his face planted in the grass—she'd been petrified-Alisha ran the Multimed close to the biggest bruise on his face. Red gave way to purple, then to yellow, until finally, the discoloration disappeared. "My head doesn't hurt anymore," he told her.

"I know. That's what's supposed to happen with this device."

He grabbed her arm with his uninjured side to halt her movement. "Should you be using this thing, then?"

"What do you mean?" She picked up his wrist and repeated the process as he'd complained about soreness there.

"If you can't use the computeller to find the arsonist, why can you use this to heal wounds?"

*Good question.* "The Guardians wanted us to have the Multimed in case we were hurt or we caused hurt to someone. Since I was with you when you got hit by that car, in a sense I caused it. If I wasn't in this time period, the accident wouldn't have happened."

"I *was* staring at your ass." He gasped. "Sorry. I didn't mean to say that out loud."

She didn't smile, frown or respond to the comment as she put the device in its black case. Then she turned to him. "I have to confess I've stared at yours, too."

"Seriously?"

"Earnestly."

He held her gaze, which burned, probably like his. "Did you like what you saw?"

"I did." A pause. "Did you?"

He nodded. Drew in a deep breath. Let it out heavily. "So what are we going to do about that, Lisha?"

Taking a seat on the kitchen chair in his home, adjacent to him, she met his gaze. "I've been thinking about that."

"So have I. I, um, wasn't sure you felt…that you were… Damn it, Alisha, are you attracted to me?"

"I'm afraid so."

"Why afraid?"

"For several reasons." Her face was marred with tense lines. "The most important one is I value your friendship and don't want to make it screwed by engaging in sex with you."

"Make it screwed? Oh, you mean screw it up."

"Whatever."

"Why do you think *engaging in sex* would hurt our relationship?"

"Because it's not natural to care about someone you join with."

His face was pale from the fall he'd taken and his eyes were shadowed. "No, you're wrong about that. The customs of *your time* are unnatural."

Transferring her gaze out the window, she didn't say anything. She could feel him watching her. Finally, she looked at him. "David, I don't want to care about a man I join with. Luke sent Dorian's head spinning when they were getting together. Celi *cried* over Alex. I can't imagine subjecting myself to that kind of emotional upheaval. I simply want to join without feelings."

"Why didn't you pursue Joe Destino then?"

She'd pondered that. And come up with no answer. None of it was logical. "I earnestly don't know. He's such a good male specimen."

"Honey, maybe you've changed. Maybe you don't really want sex without connectedness."

"No, I do. And I wish you wouldn't call me honey."

"Why?"

*Because the way you say it makes me warm inside.* "The term's insulting. It objectifies women."

"You're stretching that a bit, aren't you?"

She stood then. "No, I'm not. So please refrain." Her tone was intentionally dismissive.

"Whatever you say." His voice was harsh. And it was the first time he'd spoken to her in that tone.

"I think I'll go next door. You're tired, and it's been an eventful evening."

"Maybe that's a good idea." Still, the cold tone.

She matched it. "Fine."

Alisha left him there, sitting at the table, shoulders hunched, brow furrowed and a horrible scowl on his face. She went out the back way through the porch. Her stomach cramped, and her heart felt hollow. She marched over to her sliding doors, went inside and plopped down in the living room.

"Megadamn him," she said aloud to the empty space. "I do *not* like these feelings he engenders. I *must* stay away from him for a while."

The advice to her troubled heart didn't help. Instead, the negative feelings inside her increased. It was only six in the evening. She'd go on the computeller. Or the computer. Ah, she'd look for some life's work. She'd been right when she told David the idleness of this time wasn't good for people. That was why she was so upset and unnerved by her discussion with David.

• • •

HAVING SLEPT FITFULLY all night, David sat in his chair at his office desk staring blankly at the computer, thinking about Alisha. A knock on his door, then Lee Ann Brooks entered the room. "Are you ready to tie up the details about the September celebration?" Every fall, the church kicked off the school/church year with a special service and Sunday School.

"Sure. Have a seat."

Across from him, she began the rundown on what the committee she headed had decided, and David half listened. Lee Ann was a lovely woman inside and out, who had a partner just as nice as she. Her ideas were innovative and he'd learned a lot from her. Suddenly, he realized that she should probably have her own church, where she was in charge of a congregation.

"David, are you listening?"

"I'm afraid I'm not. I was thinking how perhaps it's time to look for your own church. You don't need me anymore." A lot of people didn't.

Now, that little gem revealed self-pity, which he never indulged in, even when he was in the war.

Her blue eyes twinkled. "Since you bought it up, I'm thinking about getting my profile together to send out to churches searching for a new minister."

He smiled. "I'll give you a great recommendation."

"Thank you. And as long as we're being honest, would you like to confide in me about what's bothering you? Lately, you've been very distracted."

He steepled his hands and thought about her suggestion. He trusted her and, what's more, believed her insights about relationships were incisive and thoughtful. Before he could respond, she added, "Does this have anything to do with that pretty woman who seems to be at the church with you a lot?"

"It does."

"She isn't a parishioner, is she?"

"No."

"So if you're interested in her, it wouldn't be unethical."

"What, do you read minds?"

"Yours, a little bit. You have this lightness about you when she's around."

"Alisha's a complicated woman."

"And you're a complicated man."

"You're right, of course. She has issues about getting involved because of how she grew up."

Lee Ann laughed. "Don't we all?" He knew her evangelical parents objected to her sexual orientation. As if she had a choice in it.

"Alisha's situation is unique."

"Do you want to get involved with her? Be honest; it's just me and you and God here."

"God isn't giving me much advice, I have to say."

"Then I will. When you meet someone special, you have to be patient."

"I'm afraid I lost my temper last night, discussing this."

"You've talked about having a relationship?"

"We *have* a relationship. A good one. We were talking about taking it past friendship. She refuses. And I don't want to hurt her with my wants and needs."

Again Lee Ann laughed. "David, you don't have to be perfect in a relationship. You're both responsible for what happens. Stay her friend and see where it goes." She winked. "I had to push Lisa a bit, if that helps."

"What if it goes where she doesn't want it to?"

"She won't do anything she doesn't want to, and you won't force her."

"Lee Ann, is it easier being in love with someone of the same sex? Do you think more alike, know what you each want more? Because I'm flummoxed about what to do."

"Sometimes it's easier. Sometimes, we don't balance each other out enough. Every relationship has its challenges. Yours is no different."

Except that the woman he cared about came from five hundred years in the future, where sex was clinical and men didn't love the women they had it with. He shook his head at the thought after Lee Ann left. His relationship with her had challenges, all right. Were they too many to overcome?

• • •

CELESTE ENTERED THE room carrying a cup of tea. The third-floor space where she'd lived before she married Alex was large, with windows with drapes billowing in the breeze, light-colored paint and pretty wood furniture. Alisha had come to Virginia yesterday because she needed to get away from New York, and Celeste had been begging her to visit. The added benefit was that her friend was inordinately knowledgeable about other people's feelings because she was a sensitive.

"Good morning." She gave Alisha the drink. "Did you sleep well?"

"I did. Your home is calm."

"With three kids? You must be in bad shape to not have noticed their chatter and demands."

"Which you love."

"I do." Celeste's smile was sun bright.

"Scoot over." Alisha moved and allowed Celi to sit next to her in bed. Suddenly, just the feel of her friend, her scent, made Alisha miss her and Dorian so much it brought—hellor, what was this?—tears to her eyes. She'd never leaked water, not once.

Celeste grasped Alisha's hand. "Don't, Celi. Don't take on my feelings."

"I won't. I promised Alex I wouldn't drain negative emotion from anyone and take it on myself while I was pregnant. But we can talk about why you're upset."

"I'm lonely," she blurted out. "When you climbed onto the bed with me, it reminded me that I miss you and Dorian so much."

"I miss you, too. You know you can move in here any time you want. Stay for a while. This entire third floor is its own dwelling."

"I'd never interfere in your life that way."

"It wouldn't be interfering. Alex has recommended it several times. He's afraid you feel left out."

"I don't want to move from New York, Celi. What I really need is a job and somebody to join with without any emotions or feelings or demands or freaking opinions on what I should do."

"Wow. Does David Ryan fit into this somehow?"

Alisha deflated. She didn't want to lie to her friend, and she was tired of handling all this by herself. In her time, women shared problems with each other. "Yes. He wants a physical relationship that involves *feelings!*"

"The cad."

"No, don't joke." Alisha's exasperated tone reflected her state of mind. "He's wrong about this. All I want is joining. Why can't anybody believe that?"

Reaching over, Celi picked up Alisha's computer from the nightstand and turned it on. "*I* believe you, which is why I've been investigating some things." When the machine booted, she opened the top and clicked into a website. "Here, look."

"RightMatch.com. What's that?"

"An online dating service."

"Celi, the people of this time look for life partners on those sites. We compared our SexLine as a further extension to them."

"No, actually, they all don't want life partners. Some of the profiles advertise the individual isn't looking to settle down. I've found a couple of men who live in Brooklyn, who seem like nice guys but are only after companionship. I think that's code for sex."

"Huh! Maybe people aren't so different now." She wondered what David would say when she told him *that*.

"Maybe. I did some background checks on them, and they are who they say." She closed the computer and added, "But before you pursue this, think long and hard if it's what you want. I can't imagine going back to simple joining. What I have now is so wonderful, it's inexplicable."

"Dorian, too. But I don't think that kind of life is for me."

"All right. Let's look at some potential partners."

Alisha agreed. This would be a good thing to do. This was what she wanted. This was better than messy sex with David. It would keep her from *having* messy sex with David.

Only she couldn't understand why the notion made her even sadder.

# CHAPTER 8

DAVID KNOCKED ON Alisha's front door bearing gifts. She'd taken off for Virginia right after their tiff and he hadn't seen her in a few days. At least she'd texted him to tell him where she'd gone, or he would have been frantic. As any friend would.

When she didn't answer, he rang the doorbell. He'd heard her come home early this morning, and her car was still in the driveway. She opened the door on the second buzz.

And his mouth gaped. Oh, dear God in heaven. "What... what did you do to yourself?"

"Hello to you, too."

"Um, sorry." Leaning over he gave her a friendly peck on the cheek. She smelled like French perfume. "You look so different."

Self-consciously, she touched her hair. It wasn't shorter, just lighter and fuller. "Celi and I had our hair done, I think is the term. It took hours" — she held up fingernails that had been painted coral to match her dress — "for that and things called mannies and peddies, but I like the results. Don't you?"

If he liked them anymore, he'd throw her over his shoulder and carry her upstairs, against her will if he had to. Lee Ann might have been wrong about his not forcing anything on her. "I do."

"Come on in. I have an hour before I have to leave."

She led him to the living room, where they sat in the warm breeze drifting from the front to the back. For a moment, he was distracted by her crossed legs. She wore strappy sandals as she had the night she went out with Joe. "Where are you going?"

"I have a date."

David swallowed hard. He'd never expected this. "With Destino again?" he croaked out.

"No." Hell, she even had makeup on—her lashes were thicker and her mouth covered in lipstick. "I have a date with a medical physician named Eric King. He seems like a very nice man online."

"Fuck it, Alisha, you went to an online dating site? Those things are dangerous. Predators—"

She had the gall to hold up her hand to stop him. "Celi checked him out on the computeller. His wife died a year ago and he's just looking for a casual relationship."

David lifted an eyebrow. "As in meaningless sex."

"Celi said that's the code."

"It is."

Squirming some, she nodded to the folder he carried. "What's that?"

Briefly, he hesitated. "It's why I came over. I missed you while you were gone and did some research."

"On what?"

"A job for you."

"Earnestly? How sweet."

"There are a lot of different prospects for anthropology jobs in the city, and some here in Brooklyn, too. I thought maybe we could go over them together and try to get you some interviews."

"That would be very helpful. Thanks."

He grasped her hand and she let him. Actually, she held on. "I also want to say I'm sorry for what happened between us before you left."

"I seek your forgiveness, too. We raised our voices and were harsh with one another."

"Emotions were running high." He smiled sadly. "Which was your point, men and women getting close, right?"

"I suppose. But I felt bad for having spoken to you that way. I care very much for you, David. Very much."

"I feel the same."

She nodded to the papers. "Can I see those?"

"Um, sure." He laid them out on the table.

They were analyzing the market when the doorbell rang. David felt his heart leap in his chest. Then catapult into his stomach.

"That must be Eric. I'm afraid I have to go." She stood, and the material of her dress clung to her.

Without thinking, without his usual circumspection, he grabbed her hand again. "Don't, Alisha, don't go on that date. Please."

"What? Why?"

"Stay here with me," he blurted out. "Join with me."

Her face, which had been light and expectant, fell. "No, David, we already discussed this."

He simply couldn't let her go to another man. "We didn't talk about a compromise."

"I don't understand." The doorbell rang again. "David, I must—"

Standing now, he grabbed her arms. "Friends often have recreational sex without it spilling over into romance. Why don't we give that a try?"

109

• • •

A SENSE OF relief swept through Alisha, shocking her. She thought she'd been looking forward to a date with Eric King — she'd convinced herself of it — but as soon as she saw David at her door, she'd wished he'd come to share the evening with her, not the doctor, whom she'd met yesterday for coffee, who was nice, but who was just another man.

Which she thought she wanted.

So she said eagerly, "Define recreational sex."

His eyes widened as if he'd expected her to object. Then a broad smile spread across his face. "Fun sex without commitment. It's close to what you had in your future."

The doorbell was shrill to her ears this time.

"Do you think we can do it that way?"

"We can try. I'm game if you are."

"Willing to try?" He nodded. "All right."

Another peal of the bell. "What do I tell Eric?"

They came up with a story, and Alisha answered the door. A very handsome man with blond hair and green eyes stood before her. He said, "Hello, again."

But she felt no spark of need. So she stepped outside, closed the door and said, "Hi, Eric. I'm sorry, I'm not going to be able to go with you tonight."

When she came back in, she found David by the dining-room windows, staring out, sipping a glass of white wine. She didn't have any in her home. "You went back to your place to get that?"

Turning, he faced her. "And to pick up a few things."

She noticed the second glass on the table. "Thanks for pouring me some." Picking it up, she sipped it. There was a bag on the table, too. "What's in that?"

"Condoms, for one."

"The archaic method of controlling reproduction? We won't need—" She halted her protest. "I suppose we might. Celi's pregnant and Dorian hopes to be soon. I do not."

"Which is why I got them." He rolled his eyes. "I can't wait for your reaction when you see what they look like."

She laughed out loud. "Are you feeling…shy, or doubtful about this?"

"Not in the least." His expression was smug.

"Me, either," she responded eagerly. "I want it."

"To join."

"Yes, I've been without sex over five months."

"How does it work in your time? What exactly is the process? I heard the others joke about multiple orgasms, and such, but walk me through it."

*Tell him ahead of time.* "The chosen place of meeting is up to the caller. We do not join in one of our dwellings. We go to a neutral room…a hotel, I think you'd call it in your time."

He dug into his pocket and brought out his keys. "Then come, let's head out."

"What? Where?"

"We're going to do this like you do in the future. There's a hotel about a half hour from here." The keys jangled in his hand. "We can't frequent a place near my church."

"David, I don't think that's necessary."

"Yep, doll, it is."

Surprised at his insistence and how he took over, Alisha followed him to his vehicle and sat beside him on the drive. She liked the radio box and asked for musicals. He picked some by the instrument saxophone. "This is pleasing."

"I play the sax."

"Earnestly? I'd love to hear you make musicals."

Reaching over, he put his hand on her knee. "In our other life, I'll play for you."

Though the situation was odd, it was also exciting. The headlights put his face in sharp relief and he looked relaxed. As though he wasn't under any pressure. She felt the urge to tease.

"In my time, there's reciprocal release. Several times."

He winked at her. "I'll try to keep up. And if I can't, I'm sure you know enough about extending the experience for both of us."

"I think the word is *touché*."

When they reached the hotel, he ushered her inside, rented a room, and they rode the elevator up. Alisha shifted from one foot to another. Her excitement grew and she couldn't stand still. What kind of a joiner would David be? Skilled? Sensual? Tender? The last had no place in joining, so she hoped he wasn't.

Once inside the room, he walked to the set of drawers and set down the bag and the wine he'd packaged up. From inside, he drew out two of those neck things Jess and Luke sometimes wore.

"What are those for?"

"Assistance. In doing this your way."

Alisha remembered Celeste reading a wildly popular novel and telling her about it. "In my time, we don't imitate what goes on in the book titled *Sixty Shades of Something*."

His grin was and wasn't David's. It was that of a man who knew his mind and was enjoying himself. "This isn't for bondage; it's a blindfold."

She glanced at the windows. "That can't mean anything to do with those."

"To cover our eyes. That way, we can be anonymous."

"I see."

"So, do you disrobe each other?"

"No, never. Though Dorian says it's very sensual. In my time, we both shed our own clothes."

"Do you watch each other?" he said, unbuttoning his shirt. Chest hair and muscles peeked out, ones she'd seen — admired — before.

"I...hadn't thought about it. I guess we don't." Which was disappointing. Suddenly, she wanted to see him strip. For her.

"Go ahead, then. Let's proceed." His language mirrored her sometimes more formal diction.

Reaching down, Alisha drew up the dress and slid it over her head. He'd dropped his shirt and his muscles seemed larger than she remembered from when she'd seen him bare chested the night he played basketball. His hands were on his shorts but stopped when his gaze caught on her. "Wow!"

She cocked her head, then realized she stood before him in the skimpy, black underclothing Celi had bought for her. Pure female joy suffused her. She wasn't shy, either. She stood there, hoping to excite him. Again, she wondered at his capabilities. He was a minister, after all.

Reaching to the front, she unclasped the silly, uncomfortable garment called a bra and let it fall to the floor.

David swallowed hard.

Then she inched down the almost-nothing bottoms.

He closed his eyes. "Oh, God, I hope I last."

"Premature ejaculation is common in your time. I know how to prevent it."

"I'll manage myself, thanks." Holding her gaze, he unzipped his pants and kicked off his shoes and shed the rest of his clothing. In the process, his genital part leaped out at her.

She smiled.

The bag crinkled as he reached for it again, pulled out the box and removed a condom. His hands shook as he brought it to his groin. Started to roll it on.

"Does that hurt?"

"Um, no."

He fumbled.

"What does it feel like?"

"Alisha, just be quiet and let me do this. I'm having enough of a hard time, you're so gorgeous and desirable."

She was about to tell him complements weren't exchanged in joining, then he finally got the thing on. And she burst out laughing.

"What?"

"I've never seen a male genital part with a coat on."

"Very funny. You know the kids call them raincoats."

"I'm sure they get wet."

"Stop!" He turned and picked up the blindfolds. "Come over here."

She approached him. From deep inside her, she felt the urge to sidle up to him, slide her arms around his neck and mate their mouths. Not entirely under control, she started to.

"Uh-uh. No kissing. This is pure joining."

"Oh." She'd forgotten.

He led her to the bed, urged her to sit. He secured the cloth around her eyes. After a moment he said, "Now stretch out." She obeyed.

His weight pressed into the bed. "I've got my eyes covered now." He moved and she felt him beside her. "Can I touch you, all over?"

"Yes. By the godheads, yes."

He started with his mouth on her neck. It was warm and wet, and she jerked when his tongue invaded her ear, because without the ability to see, the action was a hundred times more intense. Her breasts ached. When he ran his hands up and down her arms, she shivered. When he slid them around her front, played with her navel she moaned. His hand drifted farther down, to her groin, but he exerted no pressure. "David..."

"Do people of your time tell each other what they want?"

"Sometimes. Touch me there, hard."

He ground his palm into her, and she ricocheted into him. "Like this?"

"Y-yes."

His hand made circular motions, and she felt the spirals begin. In her time, reaching the peak only occurred when two people were joined, but she couldn't stop him if she wanted to. Pleasure burst inside and shot out of her. It was sweet and intense at the same time. When she felt his fingers slide into her, the pressure started to build again before the aftershocks of the first subsided. This time the coming was hot and hard and acute. She shouted out.

Her body went limp when the pleasure subsided. He raised his hands to her breasts and said, "Is this allowed?"

"Yes, but...."

"What?"

"Our custom was stimulation with your hands. Dorian told me men today like to put their mouths there. She said it's wonderful your way, so I'm willing."

"No, then, we can't do that. We gotta stick to the script."

"Okay. But it doesn't include sex with our mouths, either."

"Maybe we'll have to reconsider!" was all he said before he touched her again.

• • •

DAVID LAY ON the bed, still blindfolded, his hands grasping the head rails, as she worked her magic on him. He couldn't see anything, of course, but the air in the room was cool on his heated skin. She ran her palms over his chest and tweaked his nipples. He wanted to see her face as her hands moved below his waist, but a deal was a deal, and he'd said she could take the lead. He just hoped he could last.

As if she read his mind, she whispered in his ear, "It's all right to reach pleasure through my hands. I did with you."

Oh, thank God.

With the comment, she lowered her hand to his groin, but didn't grasp his penis. Instead, she went to the inner groin and...well, did something there. Intense arousal followed the slight manipulation. His cock grew granite hard. He knew they didn't talk during sex in her time, so he couldn't ask her... Oh, shit. Oh, God. "Alisha, geez."

He saw stars, blinding light; a shock went through his body to every nerve ending. He came and came and came.

Later, he felt her beside him. He was on his back, breathing like bellows. She didn't touch him, and he craved the contact but didn't ask for it.

"Can I say something?"

"Yes." She sounded breathless, too.

"Thank you. For whatever you did. I've never experienced anything like that."

"I think the term is *back at ya*."

"I'm glad. I need to keep up with my competitors."

"We take a few minutes to recover in between bouts."

Even if David hadn't been blindfolded, he would have closed his eyes and thanked, earnestly, his God.

Twenty minutes later, when he sat on the edge of the bed, she straddled him. Slowly, she eased herself down on him.

David felt her inch by inch. Felt her tight warmth encompass him. When she reached the hilt, she settled into him and sighed.

"Ah, that feels so..." He wanted to say *right* but he didn't. He'd adhere to the bargain, even if it killed him, which it just might. "Shh, no talking."

She didn't respond, but began to move. He let her, then after a minute, he grasped her hips, to guide her, to increase the pressure. His arms banded around her tightly, his chest melding with hers, and they moved fast...faster, until her spasms engendered his own. Consciousness faded in the face of the acute, almost painful release.

• • •

ALISHA AWOKE TO sun on her face. It peeked in through the blinds that they had not quite closed in their haste to get to each other. Eyes shut—they must have shed the blindfolds at some point—she reached for David. Her hand came up empty.

She turned over, enjoying the extra spongy mattress. He was not in bed with her. She glanced at the bathing space. The door was ajar, but the space, uninhabited. Scanning the room, she noted her clothes lay neatly over the chair but his were gone. All trace of him was. Then she saw a sheet of paper propped up on the table by the bed. She reached for it.

"Alisha,

I woke up at six and you were sound asleep. I assumed your people did not have morning-after sex, or pillow talk, so I left. I hope it's okay if you take a taxi home. There is money on the dresser for it. I'll be at church all day in meetings. Why don't you go over the anthropology job information I brought you and we can discuss it tonight? I'll be just your friend, plain old David, again then."

Huh! He was right, joiners never spent the night together, but she remembered collapsing into the pillows. So had he. Apparently, they'd fallen asleep.

Thinking back to the experience, she savored his scent, still surrounding her and bringing back memories of them joined. She'd reached release four times, and he, three. He obeyed all the rules, though she'd wanted his mouth everywhere that Dorian and Celeste said a man liked to put it today. She and David had done exactly what she'd asked for, and it had been stellar. Probably because she hadn't joined with a man in months.

But something niggled at her. Maybe abstinence wasn't the only reason the sex had been so good. She pushed the notion away. Mostly because, if she voiced her inner thoughts, she wouldn't be able to join with him again. She had to obey the rules, too.

With that notion firmly in her mind, she threw back the sheet and climbed out of bed, shivering in the conditioned air. Almost every muscle in her body screamed its soreness at her. But she'd craved that soreness and let herself enjoy the sensation. Time enough to get back to plain old Alisha.

• • •

*SO, THANK YOU for last night.*

God would smile at David as he sat in a pew and prayed.
*I meant what I said. I'll keep it impersonal.*

If he were God, he'd smirk. Not at David's intentions, but his ability to do what he said.

*Please help me do what I say, mean what I say and not try to trick her into something she doesn't want.*

*You won't make her do anything she doesn't want to do, David.*

David's head snapped up. Never had he heard God directly speak to him like that. "Huh?"

*You heard me. Have faith you'll do what you say. For as long as you need to.*

*Thank you. For the assurance and talking directly to me.*

*On occasion, I do. You don't remember when the first man you approved to go back into combat died. Who do you think got you through that?*

*You. But I don't remember hearing you directly.*

*Because you were a basket case.* He thought he heard a chuckle. *Alisha wouldn't know what that means.*

*Please, watch over her. I worry.*

*I am, son, I promise.* A pause. *Now go to your meeting. Those refugees need more help, and your church is able to give it to them.*

God didn't say good-bye as David left the sanctuary, its familiar scent of candles enveloping him. Of course, God wouldn't, because God was always with him. David felt that so strongly now. He smiled all the way to his office.

His own parishioners arrived for the meeting five minutes after he dropped down behind his desk. The three of them had spearheaded the church's participation in refugee resettlement. They were assigned a family from Somalia, a mother with three children under four. He knew the work was demanding.

David's smile was genuine. "Welcome. Coffee? There's Coke for you, Ron."

Ron, a retired Kodak employee, fetched drinks for him and the women. Penny, a consultant, sipped hers. She looked tired today. And Kathy, a former teacher turned author, smiled. "I love your coffee, David."

"Thanks. I want to talk about how hard this resettlement has been for you. Kathy, you said it was the most difficult volunteer work you've ever done."

"And the most satisfactory. But yes, we need more people involved."

"My daughters are willing to help," Ron stated. "But their time is limited."

Penny sighed. "I can't do more, David, with my schedule."

Now, this he was good at. Confident in his ability. "You won't have to. I've got reinforcements." He heard the door outside his office open, and some low murmurs. "And they're here right now."

Kathy raised her eyes heavenward. "Thank you, God."

In walked Kerry Mackenzie and three members of her congregation. "Right on time, Kerry." David stood. "I think I've met Patti, Wendy and Rob, right?"

The sisters and brother nodded. "Nice to see you again," Rob said. The girls greeted him, too, then they sat in a semi-circle around David's desk.

"Now," he asked his people, still feeling buzzed by his connection to God. "Can you tell us what you need?"

They discussed several things: someone to keep in contact with the boys' school, alternating the ubiquitous grocery shopping, helping the mom, Zarah, with laundry, hygiene, language.

Kerry spoke when they'd finished the list. "I have something else to add. You know I'm on the Brooklyn Ministerial Refugee Resettlement Board. We're looking for someone to introduce the children and adults to computers. David, is there an expert in your church who can fill that role?"

He thought of Alisha, not that she'd been very far from his mind since he'd left the hotel this morning—which had taken the strength of Hercules to do. "Yes, Kerry, I just might."

She stayed behind when the others left. "How are you, David? I haven't seen you around much when we have our services here." She smiled. "And you haven't called in a while."

"I'm well. Is your leg healed?"

"It is. I can go, say, dancing?"

His stomach plummeted. He knew, deep in his heart, that denying the invitation would be because of Alisha, and that it wouldn't be keeping his promise to her. To God. So he swallowed hard and said, "I'd love to go dancing. When?"

• • •

WHEN SHE RETURNED home that morning, Alisha did something she'd never done before. She took a bath in the big tub in one of the bathing rooms. The water was hot as she stepped in, and steam rose from it. She'd turned on the conditioner of air so the temperature wouldn't get uncomfortable in the house.

Lazing back while the heat worked magic on her sore muscles, she thought about what she'd do today.

*Why don't you go over the anthropology job information I brought you and we can discuss it tonight? I'll be just your friend, plain old David, again then.*

Yes, she would do that. Willingly. Gladly. She wanted work; she needed work. Having a life purpose had always sustained her. Too much idle time now was not a good thing.

Because she needed to keep thoughts of David as he'd been last night at bay. She'd never expected him to be so fun loving, so at ease, so…skilled at joining. His bit of aggressiveness had made him more attractive, which, she'd realized on the drive home, she probably shouldn't be feeling. She wondered what he was thinking this morning. Closing her eyes, she let her mind drift and her body's aches ease.

She'd just stepped out of the tub and donned a short robe when she heard her computeller buzz. She hurried to the den, concerned. Dorian, Celeste and she had agreed to phone, text or Skype these days and use the computeller only in case of emergency.

Sitting in the padded chair, she called up the device. Celeste's lovely face came on the screen. Her hair was up in some kind of knot, and she was rosy-cheeked. "Good morning," she said to Alisha.

"Good morning."

Leaning in, Celeste studied her closely. "Ah, I see I was right."

"About what?"

"I got this strong feeling that something good had happened to you last night. It wouldn't go away, so I decided to call and make sure it wasn't wishful thinking. I wanted to see your face, and I tried earlier to Skype, but couldn't reach you. So I used the computeller."

"You're a sensitive. You get a lot of feelings about people."

Celeste ignored the protest. "Who did you join with? The doctor?"

Alisha couldn't help but smile. "Well, I did have a date with him last night."

"Oh, Lisha, I'm so glad. So how was the sex?"

She wasn't really lying to her friend. She'd only misled her. "I have to say the sex was fabulous. I'm very pleased I had the opportunity and intend to seek it out again."

Her friend sighed. "What did David think of all this?"

"David?"

"Yes, you and he have become close. In truth, I thought there was more between you than friendship. But I guess I was wrong."

*No, you weren't wrong.* "David and I share a deep friendship. I hope that never changes."

"I don't know why I'm going on about this. But I love David, and I'd hoped you might find with him what I have with Alex."

"I don't want what you have with Alex, Celi. I've told you that many times."

"I know. Since you've joined with someone else, I'll let it go."

"Great. Now, tell me how the prenatal checkup went, how and if Maddy got a dress for her event in October."

The conversation with Celi lasted an hour, then Alisha dressed, ate some oatmeal, which was bland but tasty enough for her. When she finished, she went out to the patio and sat under the umbrella with the job information David had given her. She'd analyze it, make notes and be prepared for their discussion tonight. Maybe she'd go for a bicycle ride afterward. Maybe David would be home to accompany her. She could think of him today as just her friend—that was okay.

This was going to work out. It was! They both just had to be disciplined.

• • •

OKAY, SO DAVID hadn't been disciplined enough to stop the invitation to Alisha to meet him at the bar in the Brockman Hotel that night. He'd repressed thoughts of her all day, so he felt he deserved this.

He'd texted her: *Bring the papers to the bar at the hotel. About six. We'll be David and Alisha — friends — and work out some options for potential jobs. Then, if we both want reciprocal release, we can go upstairs as strangers.*

Must be he wasn't out of line because she'd texted right back, *Yes.*

She appeared at the entryway to the bar, and his body immediately responded to the sight of her. As she walked toward him, he noted she wore white slacks and a navy top that dipped in the front with some kind of ruffle. Her hair looked freshly washed and her cheeks glowed. She reached him. "Hello."

Rising, he kissed her cheek. "Hello."

When they both sat, he asked, "This was okay, wasn't it?"

"Talking about the job?" Her eyes twinkled with her tease. "Of course."

He shook his head.

"Or do you mean joining after? Yes. I've often participated in multiple nights of joining."

The smile he gave her was phony because the thought of her with those anonymous men made him sad. He had to control his reactions if he was going to be in this relationship on her terms. "I guess I've done that, too." A long time ago. "So, let's look the job situation in the vicinity for anthropologists."

"The good news is," Alisha said as she took out her pocket computer and called up her notes. "There's a predicted twenty-one percent rise in the need for anthropologists in the near future."

David sat back and listened. "That's terrific. What are some specific jobs in the field?

"One is with your Department of Defense." She shook her head at the notion that countries went to war these days. If they'd only known… "They hire people to study the customs of a variety of regions, probably that they hope to invade!"

"I think that one's out for you. You won't even kill a spider."

"We're all peace loving in the future."

"I know. And admire that."

When she glanced back down, he noticed her hair fell into her eyes. Its golden strands, put there by a hairdresser, sparkled in the light from the windows. "The second is with corporations." She read aloud. "'Conglomerates employ anthropologists to understand increasingly diverse work-forces and markets, allowing businesses to better serve their clients or to target new customers.'"

"I didn't know that."

"So for both," she continued, "anthropologists examine the customs, values and social patterns of different cultures, then advise organizations and governments on the cultural impact of proposed plans, policies and programs."

"Working with businesses sounds interesting."

Alisha frowned. "Alex had a good experience with his pharmaceutical company until we changed his findings."

"Jess works for Vista Institute. He likes that."

"Still, I don't find the government or big business appealing."

Man, he'd been hoping he could help her flesh out her life. "Was there anything you did like in that information?"

"Yes." She clicked some keys. The Museum of Anthro-pological Studies in Manhattan has received a five-million-dollar grant to fund a new project called *Bridging the Gap from the Past to the Future.*"

"Seriously? That sounds right up your alley."

At her blank look, he explained the term.

"They're in need of…" Here she read aloud again. "'…a person to oversee projects, which are in various stages of research, and analyze the data with an eye to predicting the future of society. Our hope is to alert people to the effect of their actions. A PhD and previous field work are required.'"

"You can take care of credentials with your computeller, right?"

"Yes, though in truth, I've had extensive field work and equivalent training in my time."

Leaning over, he chucked her under her chin. "You are smart, Lisha. I'll give you that."

Their first task would be getting a list of the projects that would be overseen, then establish the right background and education. They discussed interviewing, which Alisha had reservations about.

"Celi and Dorian say sometimes I can be cold."

He took a gulp of wine. And sometimes so hot she blew the top of his head off.

"I think you're warming up to everything in society."

She gave him a sideways glance.

"We can set up some practice interviews. Tell me, are you happy about the possibility of doing work you like?"

"Of course. I need to occupy my mind, and this is a good cause. It will help others."

"That's my main goal, too, in my ministry." He studied her. "What are you thinking?"

"I'm thinking of one of the theories of time travel — that if people go back to the past and change it, that they were meant all along to be here and alter the present."

"Yes," he said dryly. "I remember talking about it when Alex needed convincing."

"It's a paradox, but—" She cut herself off, probably realizing this argument could be used to convince her she should find the arsonist in the computeller chips. He wouldn't ask, though.

He gestured to her computer. "And you wonder if you were meant to have this job?"

She nodded.

"You *were* sent here to change things." He let the comment hang, then made a quick decision to table the discussion. "Well, I guess that finishes this part of the night."

"The David-and-Alisha-as-friends part."

"Uh-huh."

Music filtered out from speakers in the bar—some bluesy jazz. The lights had dimmed. They stared at each other.

David decided to take the reins. Standing, he fished some money from his pocket and threw it on the table. "Are you ready to go upstairs, doll?"

She couldn't help but smile. "I am."

• • •

"BLESSED LORD,

I know he's in there right now, dozing on his couch. I watched when he locked up—stupid man—and settled in for the night. He is the worst, you said, because of his liberal views. Because he's swayed so many into believing in the wrong paths. Give me grace to be patient, check his routine, and finally to follow through, to take this big step, to right the wrongs of the past. I need you in my soul to do this.

Your Servant always."

# CHAPTER 9

LUKE'S OFFICE AT the police station precinct reflected the personality of the surly, contrary man himself. There were no knickknacks, a scarred oak desk, on which sat one photo of Dorian, and shelving that was neat and organized. Right now, he stared over at Alisha, nearly making her squirm. If anyone could help her with the interview process, it was this impossible man. So what if she'd come to like him, especially since he fell in love with Dorian? He could still be a bastard.

Today, they were playing roles.

"Ms. Law. Nice to meet you."

"Thank you, Mr. Cromwell. You, too."

"So, tell me about yourself, especially anything that will affect your ability to manage the grants here at the Museum of Anthropology.

She'd already researched the common protocol of interviews on the Internet and was prepared for most questions. Basically, she stuck with the story she'd initially told everyone else. "I grew up in South America and lived there for seventeen years." She gave him an ingratiating smile. "I'm used to dealing with people from other cultures. And I speak six languages—Spanish, Italian, French." She wouldn't tell him about Prizian and Stalch, two of the new languages in the future. "Multilingualism would be help-

ful in the South American development you want to innovate in."

"*Innovate in* is awkward, Lisha. Say *to make innovations in.*"

She bit her lip. "What if I misspeak frequently, Luke?"

"Try to use all phrases you know. If you make a glaring
error, explain you spoke English as a second language."

Rolling her eyes, she sighed. "With the way you talk here,
I almost do."

A half grin turned up the corners of his mouth, making
her see why Dorian found him attractive. "We're not so bad."
Luke pretended to check some paperwork. "What was your
biggest weakness in the last position you held?"

*Turn your weaknesses into strengths*, the interview tips had
advised. So she said, "I don't like to simply meet deadlines. I prefer to reach them early. Sometimes, my staff couldn't keep up."

Luke nodded appreciatively.

After an hour of grilling, Alisha was drained, which
didn't happen much to her, though she *was* eating more of
their sustenance, and it gave her less energy. Leaning over,
Luke squeezed her hand. "You're ready, doll."

*Are you ready to go upstairs, doll?*

*I am.*

She asked, "When men use doll like that, Luke, what is
their intention?"

Luke shrugged. "To be playful. I use it to make Dorian
pissed. Sometimes, to distance a person. A lot like the negative use of lady."

She nodded.

"Why do you want to know? Your interviewer won't use
the term."

"Of course not. I'm still trying to figure things out and I
heard it on *LifeLine Television for Women.*"

Alisha brought up Dorian, and she marveled at the change in Luke's face when he talked about her. "Lisha, did you hear that? She's starting a fitness studio."

"Um, yes, I know. She decided when she has a baby, she can still run a gym but was worried she couldn't manage a real version of Masterminds."

"Man, I didn't want her chasing people around."

"Did you sway her?"

"Maybe some." At Alisha's frown, Luke added, "It's all right to let people you love influence your decisions, Lisha."

Her mind went to David and how he'd influenced her in a myriad of ways. Though it sometimes made her uncomfortable, she was a lighter, friendlier…better person with him.

"I suppose." She stood. "Thank you for doing this with me, Luke. I must leave. I have an appointment at eleven."

"With David. I talked to him last night. That's nice of you to volunteer for the refugee project."

"I haven't, yet. I'm…scoping it out."

He grinned. She grinned, and the day seemed brighter. Which was exactly what she needed.

As she took the train back to Brooklyn, she thought about why she needed…cheering up. In the last few days, she'd spent dual lives with David. He'd helped her with the interview questions but wasn't tough enough on her — did he even have that in him? Then, at the hotel, he was so intent on her, her pleasure, her well-being it warmed her even thinking about that night.

Unfortunately, she'd been lost in thoughts of them and what they'd done to each other and almost missed the Brooklyn stop. She barely made it off the train and briskly walked the block to the Center where she was meeting David.

And Reverend Kerry Mackenzie.

Who liked David, in a romantic way.

Alisha wondered if it would bother her if David was involved with Kerry? Maybe if he stopped seeing *her*. Hellor, she didn't want to think about that. But her mind wouldn't cooperate. Alisha had met Kerry on several occasions. She'd always had a possessiveness about David, something that irked Alisha, though she couldn't figure out why. Kerry seemed like a very nice woman. Were her petite stature and wholesome good looks more appealing to David than...? Megadamn. She couldn't go there.

As she approached the building, she remembered the Center had once been a school and had been converted to a charitable center for these kinds of projects. Then she saw David swing open the front door, and her heart lurched. He wore his collar and black clothing, accenting his...holiness, she guessed. But then the images of him and what he'd last done to her superimposed over that, and she was dizzy for a moment from the contrast.

He said, "Hi, there."

She placed her hand in his outstretched one and squeezed. "Hi."

"Trip back out okay?"

"Fine."

"Luke?"

"Good."

They'd entered the structure and were walking down the corridor. He leaned over and said in a low voice, "I hope we're not reduced to one-word answers when we're in friend mode."

"No, of course not. I almost missed the stop. My mind is scattered."

"Because of the job. Don't worry, you'll get the interview and we'll be celebrating soon."

Still thinking about him and his two personalities, she stopped before they got to the door. "Who will we be then, David?"

Briefly, a shadow crossed his face. His voice was rusty when he answered, "Who do you want to be?"

Their gazes locked. "I'm not sure. Let me decide then."

"There you are." Kerry had come out into the corridor, and Alisha felt a sudden surge of inadequacy.

A dress with pink coloring flattered her light complexion and reddish hair. On her feet were strappy shoes called sandals, which were appealing but not comfortable, Alisha knew from the night of her date with Joe and her non-date with the doctor. Her eyes sparkled when she looked at David, then the woman focused on her. "Hello, Alisha. Thank you for coming."

"You're welcome. But I haven't agreed to anything yet."

A really feminine chuckle escaped her. "No worries. David here"—she reached out and touched his arm—"is very convincing."

"Is he?"

They sat at a small conference table in an office that consisted of a desk, the table and not much else. Except for the stunning pictures on the walls around the room. Pointing to them, she asked, "Are all of these refugees?"

"Yes, and more arrive every month."

"From war-ravaged areas?"

"Or occupied ones. Many of them escape from camps."

Alisha had researched refugee camps. Not only did these people go to war, but they persecuted innocent victims during and after. "Those places are horrible."

"Which is why we're here to help anyone who manages to get free."

ANOTHER TIME

David had sat by listening. "Why don't you tell Alisha about the training you want her to do?"

Kerry gave him a lovely smile, then transferred her gaze to Alisha. "We'd like you to teach groups of children how to use computers. If you enjoy that, we can go on to adults. But our children are far behind in school because of their lack of tech skills. David said you can take a computer apart and put it back together."

"I can fix any of them, if that's what you want."

"They *are* old. But he also said you'd make a good teacher."

She was about to decline, saying she had no experience in instruction, when a little boy with dark skin ran into the room. "Reverend Kerry!" He rushed over and hugged her.

"Hello, Abdefatah. How are you today?"

"Good. Can we play Upside Down after our lesson?"

"Yes, of course. Now say hello to our visitors."

The boy stepped away and held out his hand to shake Alisha's. Suddenly, she was bombarded by some of the research she'd done on refugees. Squalid conditions. Not enough food. Beaten—even children—for no reason. "Very nice to meet you, Abdefatah. Where are you from?"

His little brow furrowed. "Far away."

Without thinking, Alisha said, "So am I."

"Did you come to the Americas to be safe?"

"Not exactly. But I know what it means to leave everything you've ever known and transport to another country."

He put his hand on his heart. "I miss my grandma."

She saw David's eyes go dim and the shake his head. To the boy, she added, "I miss people I used to know, too."

Abdefatah moved in closer. "Maybe we can be friends."

"Of course we can. I'd like that."

When Abdefatah was sent to his English room, Kerry turned to Alisha. "You were wonderful with him. I didn't know you were a refugee."

"I wasn't seeking asylum, but I did come from another world."

David interrupted. "We were discussing whether or not you could help these little ones."

"Maybe I can convince you —" Kerry began.

But Alisha interrupted. "You don't have to." She looked after where the child had gone. "I'll do it."

Kerry beamed. "Oh, wow, that's just great. Thank you so much."

When they were leaving — David would drive Alisha home — Kerry snagged David's arm at the exit. "So, you never called about the dancing."

Alisha stilled.

"I know. Lots to do. I'll check my calendar and get back to you today."

"I can't wait." Standing on tiptoes, she kissed his cheek.

Alisha's heart sank in her chest, and her euphoric mood evaporated. So much so, she couldn't talk on the way to the car, couldn't enjoy the balmy mid-September air.

Once inside the vehicle, he didn't start the engine. He angled around in his seat and captured her gaze. "Kerry asked me out."

"I gathered that."

"You and I didn't talk about seeing others."

"That's encouraged in my society."

"Will that be one of the rules?" Then he snapped, "Maybe we should keep a list."

Her temper rose, too. "Are you angry about something?"

He ran a hand through his hair, messing his curls. "No, of course not." Sticking the key into the engine, he asked, "What could I be angry about? It's every guy's fantasy to have frequent, meaningless sex."

Meaningless? It had meant something to her, despite the rules. But she didn't voice her feelings. She didn't want to talk about this right now. In the mood David was in, she thought he might cancel their deal.

And Alisha wasn't ready for that to happen.

•  •  •

DAVID KNEW HE was being unreasonable—he'd agreed to her terms, after all; he'd agreed to the *just-sex* mandate. But a lot had happened earlier that Alisha didn't know about, and he wasn't in control. Which was why he pulled up in front of the Brockman Hotel instead of driving them home. He shut off the engine. Sat there. Then, staring through the front window, asked, "This okay?"

"Yes. I have time today."

When he turned to face her, his eyes were blazing with something dark and dangerous. "Do you want to?"

She held his gaze. "Very much."

They exited the car at the same time. He held the hotel door for her and she stepped ahead of him into the reception area. Waited while he secured a room. Neither spoke on the trip up to 413. Once there, he stepped aside to allow her to go in first, then shut the door behind him with uncustomary force and grabbed her arm roughly. Her brows rose and she opened her mouth.

"No, don't say anything." Despite the caveat she'd given him before about undressing, he tore open her blouse and dragged it off her. He made short work of her dress slacks and panties. Then he pushed her into the wall.

"Aren't you going to…"

Again, he silenced her, this time with his palm on her mouth. "Don't talk."

She didn't; truthfully, his aggression aroused her. Immensely. Sliding his hand between them, he realized he was still dressed. Tough. He yanked at his belt and opened his fly. Released himself. Then ground his hand against her groin. In a few seconds she said, "I'm ready. Now!"

Lifting her up, he said in a ravaged voice, "Wrap your legs around me."

She obeyed.

Then he thrust into her, pounded into her, until he couldn't see straight, think at all or even breathe.

When he came back to reality, he could feel her pressed against him, her breath fast, her legs still locked at his waist.

He realized what he'd done and slapped his hand on the wall. "Sweet Jesus." He drew back. "Are you all right?"

She looked him with…a smile. "I am. Are you?"

"I guess." He watched her. Then stepped back, so she could slide her legs to the floor. "Well, then." He picked her up.

"What are you doing?" she laughed.

Turning he crossed the room and tossed her on the bed. "I'm not done with you yet."

She came up on her arms. "Then you'd better take your clothes off." Her eyes dropped below his chin and narrowed. "David, you have your clerical collar on."

Which he was wearing when he'd rented a hotel room and practically attacked a woman. The notion didn't stop him from undressing.

Neither of them remembered until later that they'd used no contraception.

• • •

EXHAUSTED, ALISHA ENTERED her half of the house. It was freezing cold and she turned off the air conditioner and started to open the windows. When she glanced down at her

upper arms, she noticed the bruises there, given to her by the gentlest man she'd ever known. For the hundredth time, she wondered if she was a bad influence on him.

Of course she was. She'd willingly gone into a relationship with him that she knew went totally against his morals and beliefs.

Fuck!

Instead of dwelling on that, she made herself think about the interview practice with Luke. It had gone well. A few days ago she'd sent in her application and was hoping the Museum would call and request a meeting. David had helped her with the forms, Celeste and Dorian and Alex with establishing credentials. Nothing to do now but wait.

She caught sight of her computer on the table. Thinking of Abdefatah, she went online to pursue something she'd thought of earlier but hadn't shared with Kerry or David. Clicking into a local retail store, she followed the prompts and searched for what she wanted.

When her cell phone rang, she was surprised to see how much time had passed. She didn't recognize the name of the caller. She clicked on. "Alisha Law."

"Ms. Law, this is Damien Riggs." At her silence he added, "The personnel director for the Museum of Anthropology."

Her heartbeat sped up. "Yes, Mr. Riggs."

"We're very impressed with your résumé and application. We'd like you to come in for an interview. We received many applicants; yours was the last. We're interviewing ten candidates."

"I see."

"But," he said with a smile that came over the phone lines, "We called you first."

"That's good news. Let me get my calendar."

• • •

AFTER DAVID DROPPED off Alisha at her half of the duplex, he headed to church. To pray. To say he was sorry for treating her so roughly. Dear Lord in heaven, what had gotten into him? His sense of guilt multiplied like the loaves and fishes when he saw a familiar, battered Volkswagen in the parking lot of the church.

Oh, fuck! He'd had an appointment set up with Paul Mason, his troubled veteran friend, and forgotten. Though Paul had snagged the job as a cook at a place David recommended, David didn't know how things were going. The last thing the poor man needed was to be waiting around for David because he'd indulged in selfish and inappropriate behavior.

Bolting out of his car and crossing the parking lot, David found Paul in the front seat, smoking.

He approached the driver's window. "Paul, I'm so sorry. I got tied up."

The guy just shrugged, but David saw accusation in his sad eyes. David had let *him* down, too.

"We used to leave the church open, but the police suggested to all local churches that we lock them after the spate of fires in the area."

"Yeah, I heard about them. We used to set fires in theater…" He trailed off. One thing David really wanted was to get him to talk about his time in Afghanistan. Counseling about that was something David knew he was good at.

"Can you stay? To catch me up on how you've been doing."

Though he didn't answer, or get out of the car, he talked. "I'm bored. Mornings at the diner aren't enough to keep me occupied all day."

"Some volunteer work might be good for you."

"I said, no churches."

"There's volunteer work everywhere, not just through churches. Like the community center where lay people work to help refugees who flee to our country." At his hesitation, David added, "You know, those little kids would love to see a real live hero."

"As if."

"Could we just talk about that possibility?"

"Not now." He threw the cigarette out the window, and David watched as he donned *the soldier mask*. "Later maybe. I'll call you, Rev." With that, he backed out of the space and sped away.

After Paul left, David went inside through the foyer and narthex. He took a seat in the sanctuary and bowed his head. Hell, he'd blown everything.

*I'm sorry. How did I get so off course?*

He didn't hear God's response.

*Are you there?*

Still, no answer. Even God wasn't talking to him now. He hadn't thought the day could get any worse, but it just had. He didn't know what he'd do if he lost the most important thing in his life.

# CHAPTER 10

BAILEY'S IRISH PUB was an icon in New York City. As David walked toward it, he couldn't help but smile. The owners—five siblings—had led interesting lives. Its namesake, Bailey, used to work with girl gangs and had married a senator who was now the vice president of the United States. She continued her work with kids as Second Lady. Her brother Aidan had married one of Bailey's Secret Service agents. He didn't know what the other brothers had done with their lives, but he'd bet it was interesting. Their stories made him wish he'd had siblings.

Just as he reached the door, he caught sight of Joe Destino jogging toward him. Joe said, "Hey, buddy. Long time no see."

"Which is what I want to talk to you about."

"I know. The arsonist has been quiet. Damned worrisome." Joe pulled open the intricately carved oak door and they went inside.

The interior was spacious. The focal point was a U-shaped mahogany bar; a piano perched in the corner and several tables were scattered throughout. As it was later in the day, the lunch crowd had come and gone, with only a few patrons remaining. Just the scent of the food made David's mouth water. When had he last eaten?

A blond woman worked behind the bar. When she looked up, her face wreathed with smiles. She ducked under an opening to the floor, rushed to Joe and threw herself at him. "Joey!"

"Hey, Sophie baby. How ya doin'?"

"Couldn't be better. I miss you."

"I miss you, too."

She stepped back and turned to David. "Hi. I'm Sophie Tyler."

Still holding her hand, Joe rolled his eyes. "You still haven't taken his name, after all this time?"

"Nope, and I won't. Liam doesn't care."

"Did I hear my name?" Behind Sophie, a man came up to them. He had short, curly hair, blue eyes with an Irish sparkle in them and a wholesomeness that David could always sense. "Hey, buddy." He gave Joe a bear hug. "It's been a while."

"Too long."

Sophie began to chatter like someone who needed to know everything all at once. "Do you like being in arson? Don't you miss the thrill of the line?"

Liam put his hand on Sophie's neck in a gesture so intimate, David's heart clutched. He knew in that instant he wanted intimacy with Alisha. Liam said, "This one would miss the excitement of firefighting."

"You know I don't miss the line. This arson stuff's complicated." He glanced at David. "I do miss you and the guys, though."

"Let's get you a seat." Liam showed him to a table by the front window, where they could watch the streets of the Village parade by. Sophie waved to him as she went back behind the bar.

Looking after her, David remarked, "I can see she's not your girl, but she sure seems to like you."

"We hooked up a lotta years ago."

"I take it she's a firefighter."

"Yeah, but I wonder for how long. I heard she wants to have a baby."

A baby. Would David ever be a father? The image of Alisha, her body swollen with his child, flashed through his mind. He squelched it immediately.

Liam returned with the menu. "The boxy are the special. I cooked them myself."

Joe told David, "Stuffed-potato pancakes." He asked Liam, "What kind?"

"You can have a sampling of each — chicken, shrimp, sausage, portabella."

"Fine by me."

"Me, too. And beer," David told him.

"We'll have a pitcher."

Why not? It was Joe's day off and David's, too. Neither was driving. When the beer came, David drank heartily. Joe watched him. "You're worried."

"Aren't you? The arsonist has been silent for weeks. I wish I could say he's stopped, but I don't believe that."

"With good reason. Arsonists take breaks. Often they reappear."

"Do they ever just go away?"

"Yeah. But I got a feeling about this one. There's something about him hitting churches that makes me think grudges, and those ebb and flow. Something could happen to start him up again."

David sighed. "I was hoping for better news."

"I hear ya. We've kept the case open, but we have no leads."

"Damn it."

The food came, and David forced himself to eat. Nothing seemed to be going right.

"So, how's Alisha?"

*Oh, godheads, right there. Yes, David.*

"She's great." He ran a finger around the rim of his glass. "Sorry it didn't work out for you two."

"Yeah, me, too. I got the feeling there was somebody else she was thinking about."

"Not that I know of."

"It seemed like that to me. But if not, maybe I'll try again."

"She barfed all over you. You must really like her."

"I'd *like* to get her in bed."

*Hell, Alisha. Faster.*

David gave him a phony smile. "I understand that."

"Do you, David?"

"What do you mean?"

"There's something between you two, isn't there? She talked about you as if you hung the moon."

"We're friends. I like her. And she doesn't have many people in her life." He nodded to the other side of the pub. "There's a pool table over there."

"Yeah?" Joe grinned. "I used to beat the pants off you at the base."

"Funny, I don't remember it that way."

"You got a faulty memory, old man."

He wished he did.

*I can hardly move. Can we take a breather?*

*Nope. We only got an hour.*

She'd been lying on top of him one of the times they'd met at the hotel, had sex, didn't talk much. At home, they'd been cordial to each other but didn't share important things. David had engineered that. He needed to get his equilibrium back. He needed to do something to get out of this funk he'd been in since he'd attacked her in the room the day she agreed to help with the refugees.

• • •

ALISHA MISSED HER friend David. She'd been with his alter ego, but they'd shared only their bodies. So after she slid the pan of Helen's lasagna into the oven and set the timer for an hour, she went by way of the backyard to his place. It was six at night and already, she could hear sounds of the creatures who came out after dark. She'd didn't think she'd ever get used to insects and wildlife. At the door to his lovely porch she'd yet to use without him, she found him sound asleep on the couch. Standing outside the screen, she watched him. On his back, one arm raised over his head, he was snoring lightly. His curly hair was messy, and a growth of beard on his jaw had grown back. Again, he wore tight jeans and a shiny-looking, white shirt.

A hawk flew by overhead, squawking like a ducko, and David stirred. She waited to see if he'd awaken. He did—he blinked and focused on her. A very male smile. "I was just dreaming about you."

Uh-oh. The notion pleased her too much. She stepped inside. "Earnestly? What sexual gymnastics were we doing this time?"

His eyes narrowed on her. "None. We were bike riding out by the lake."

"That sounds wonderful." She glanced outside. "It's good weather this evening. Seventy-five degrees and zero humidity. Want to go for a ride now?"

Sitting up, he ran a hand over his jaw. "I'd love to. But I had a bit too much beer at lunch, and I'm still not completely sober. I'd probably flip over the handlebars."

"You've been there, done that."

He smiled at the idiom she'd gotten right.

"Tomorrow morning, then?"

"Yeah, sure." He nodded to the door. "Did you want something? Is that why you're here?"

"Oh, yeah. I made that Italian dish you like so much."

"Helen's lasagna?"

"Yep. I'm inviting you for dinner. I thought afterwards, we might come back to your place and see if there are more of those *Outer Limits* shows on the video box." She'd really enjoyed that particular entertainment's future predictions.

He struggled to his feet. "Aw, I'd love to. But I have plans tonight."

"Plans?"

"Um, a date." At her blank look, he added, "With Kerry Mackenzie. We're going dancing."

She stepped back. "You don't have to explain. I understand. You and I have an agreement."

"I'm sorry to miss the meal. Can I take a rain check?" Whatever the hellor that meant.

"Can we do it another time?"

Feigning disinterest, she raised her chin. "Maybe. If I don't eat it all tonight."

"You'll get sick. By the way, I saw Joe today."

"Is he the one you drank the beer with?"

"Yes. He said to say hello."

"Anything else?"

"That he'd wished your date went better, but he had a feeling you were thinking about another man the whole time."

"How silly. I wasn't. I ate the wrong things."

David's hands curled at his sides. "You said he was tedious, and you didn't enjoy talking to him."

"It was a bad night all around." She winked. "Maybe I'll call him. With that name, I'll bet he likes Italian food."

"I'll bet." His words were clipped.

"I'll let you get ready for your date with Kerry."

"Yeah, sure."

Turning, Alisha stepped outside. She'd gotten halfway to her house when she looked over her shoulder. David stood by a screen, watching her.

And Alisha wondered if he felt as bad as she did.

• • •

THE FOLLOWING DAY, David wondered if the chill in the air was bothering Alisha. He watched her from across the lawn, where the picnic held for the refugees was in full swing. He waved to Hal Hanson, whose church was also participating. In attendance were sixty refugees from four surrounding locales and about twenty-five workers. He'd brought three of them.

When David had gone to church before the picnic, he'd found Jase Carpenter in the backyard. The young boy was wandering aimlessly around the blacktop and grass. Going out through his office door, David called to him. "Hey, Jase. Good to see you. What're you doing here?"

Jase shrugged.

David approached him, and he noticed the bleak expression in Jase's eyes. "Problem with your parents again?"

"Is the Pope Catholic?"

Jase was.

He gave the boy a sympathetic smile. "Another fight?"

"No, the cold shoulder. Every time I won't do something they want, the don't talk to me. Fuck, I hate that more than their yelling, and they know it."

"What did they want you to do?"

"Take the daughter of one of their friends to the Fall Festival at the country club. It's a like a prom. I said no. I'm done with those things. They're so lame."

David suspected Jase didn't want to go because he was gay and sick of playing the pretend game. David had asked God if he should bring up the kid's sexual orientation, as Jase had never talked about it, and he felt the answer: when it was time, David would know what to do.

Sometimes, he wished God could be more specific. But at least, God was talking to him.

Meanwhile, he'd invited Jase to come to the picnic with him.

He surveyed his other successes, at least for today. Paul Mason was about twenty yards away. Right now, the army vet was sitting on a picnic table with a man from Somalia, deep in discussion. When David had called to remind Paul about the picnic, he'd seemed in a pretty good mood and agreed to meet David here.

"Hey, David." Jeb Morse had approached him. "How's it going?"

"Good for me." Jeb had a pleasant demeanor, which was good for clergy.

"I've been thinking about your new assistant pastorship at Universalist. Is it what you thought it would be?"

For a moment, some uncharacteristically dark emotions flitted through Jeb's eyes. "The people are great and I appreciate the work. It's just...humbling."

"I'm sorry."

"I sure hope God knows what He's doing."

David chuckled. "Don't we all."

Brian Young joined them, carrying sodas for him and Jeb. David had heard Brian had rented a room in his house to Jeb for monetary reasons. "Hey, Brian."

"David. This refugee project is great. How long have you been involved in it?"

"Over a year. My church people are resettling a family."

"It's challenging work." Brian scanned the area, his gaze landing on Jase, who sat with two little boys on his knees. "Your young friend over there seemed very excited about it. We had a good conversation today." He shrugged "I've put my name on the volunteer list."

"That's super. I'm sure you'll get satisfaction from working with the families."

"I hope so." He socked David in the arm. "I'm doing a lot better. Don't worry about me."

"I won't." Which was a lie, he thought as Kerry came over and dragged the men off to meet a family.

David headed toward a group of children who were surrounding Alisha—the third person who'd come along with him. Since many of the kids didn't speak English, he wondered how she was keeping them entertained.

When he reached them, he saw she'd placed her laptop in the center of the picnic table, with the kids gathered behind her. On the screen, fireworks erupted. Oohs and ahs in any language were pretty much the same. David smiled down at her. Just then she looked up, and the expression of joy in her eyes was so great, it poleaxed him. "These are beautiful," she said to him.

*So are you.* "The kids seem to like the show."

She swung her feet over the bench and stood. "I'm looking forward to working with them next week."

"You'll have to juggle your schedule if you get the museum job."

Another smile. She seemed relaxed and happy today. More relaxed and happy than he was. "I'm excited about that, too." She stared at him. "Looks like everything is falling into place."

*Except us.* Yesterday, when he'd been dreaming about her, then woke to find her at the porch, he'd known a longing so intense that it took his breath away. After she left, he admitted to himself and God that he wasn't sure he could continue seeing her as strangers and keep his feelings at bay.

Her gaze shifted past his shoulder. He tracked it and saw Kerry talking with Paul Mason and another man. She asked, "So, how was dancing last night?"

"Fun, though I was exhausted. I cut the evening short, came home and crashed again. That'll teach me to drink beer at lunch."

In fact, he'd gotten away from Kerry as soon as he could and wondered why the hell he'd gone out with her in the first place. He held Alisha's gaze. "Did you call Destino?"

"Um, no. I didn't." She bit her lip. "I saved the food. For you. Want to come over tonight? I know it's Saturday, but we can eat early so you get enough rest for tomorrow."

Reaching out to squeeze her arm, he said meaningfully, "It's a date."

Kerry approached them, smiling. She wasn't smiling at the end of last night, though. "Hey, you two. I have good, good news. The top administrator for the ministerial board for the project said twelve brand new laptops will be delivered to us Monday morning." She bestowed a grin on Alisha. "So you'll have up-to-date equipment to work with."

"How wonderful."

"Where did they come from?" David asked.

"An anonymous donor. I wish he'd told us who he is though. I'd love to thank him."

"I'm sure he knows how much you needed them." This from Alisha.

When Kerry left, David watched her. "Huh! Isn't that interesting? You're getting brand new machines to work on. I wonder who donated them."

One of the kids tugged on her arm. "Oh, look, the show's over. I have to find something else for the kids. Tonight, about six?"

"Yeah, sure, I'll see you then."

She walked away and he smiled after her. Maybe he was happier today than he realized.

• • •

ALISHA KNEW SHE was getting used to this time period when the smell of lasagna heating in the oven stirred her appetite. She was certainly used to the outdoors—she didn't ever call it out of inside anymore—and had gone on a long bike ride by herself today. She hadn't asked David to come along. As she was musing in the kitchen, he came to the screen doors and knocked, then opened one. She adored the coolness of the September air and had left off the air-conditioning once again.

"Man, that smells good."

"I was just thinking the same thing." She went to the counter and poured them some red wine, another thing she was liking these days.

"That's a big step for you. Are the supplements gone?"

"Yes. It's okay, though. I watch what I eat, but I'm splurging tonight. I think my body-fat index is still at zero."

"I can attest to that."

Memories of how he knew that made her warm, so she said, "Have some wine. Let's go outside and drink it."

They settled under the umbrella. "The refugee picnic was fun." She grinned. "Those younglings are...adorable."

150

"They seem taken with you. It'll help when you start teaching them on your new computers."

Looking away, she stared off into the yard.

"Don't bother denying it. I know you bought them. You wanted to do the same for the church."

She shrugged. "I thought they should learn on current machines, no matter how archaic even the new ones are."

"You were very generous."

"We're not running out of diamonds anytime soon. Dorian and Celi don't use any."

"Still, it was a nice gesture."

The timer rang, and Alisha left to remove the dinner from the oven. She set up the meal on the patio, and they ate—he with gusto, she with some restraint. It was pleasurable to watch him enjoy himself so much. "David, you have a lot of responsibility."

"Why yes, I do. Where did that come from?"

"I was thinking about all the people you brought to the picnic today. And I can tell you're trying to help the two men whose churches closed."

"That's my job, Lisha. To help others."

"We believed that it was everyone's job in my time."

"And still you didn't believe in *God*."

"You don't need to believe in religion or God to do good work."

"Do you ever wonder if there's religion in the future now, after you've changed it?"

"Assuming we've changed it. I wish there was some way to know."

"Have faith."

She rolled her eyes. "Truthfully, I'm not sure I want that to have changed. Religion has caused your society great problems."

"Ah, but God adds so much to our lives. I can't imagine a world without God in it."

"I bought dessert." She wanted to change the subject.

He rubbed his hands on his belly. "You're ruining my waistline, woman."

She arched a brow at him. "I can attest to that not being true, too, David."

The innuendo, and invitation, came out in the tone of her voice. So he asked, "Are you thinking you'd like to join tonight, Alisha?"

"Yes." She frowned. "But it's getting later and you wanted to turn in early. The hotel is a good thirty minutes away, and then back."

"I know."

The look they exchanged was meaningful.

"It's becoming an ass pain to go there, David."

He laughed heartily. "A *pain in the ass*, honey. And yes, I agree."

"Do you think we can dispense with that requirement?"

The expression in his eyes turned heartfelt. "Alisha, maybe we should—"

She stood abruptly, afraid that he would say something to ruin their arrangement. Holding out her hand, she said, "Let's go to my sleeping space. I think the bed is big enough for you."

"For us."

The phrase was ominous, but she let it go and led him to the bedroom.

• • •

FEELING LIKE A hypocrite, David nonetheless went with Alisha to the bedroom. The blinds were slatted, the room dim in the early evening. She didn't turn on any lights, making the setting romantic. Her scent rose to greet him even more intensely—flowery, sweet.

He shouldn't be thinking those things, nor the notion that he wanted to kiss her more than he wanted intercourse. Despite tonight's dispensation, he had to stay as true as he could to the agreement.

Or stop making love to her.

"Why do you look so sad? Are you too tired for this?"

He dropped his shorts and briefs. "Do I look too tired?"

She gave him a siren's smile. "Oh, good." And removed the rest of her clothes.

Zero body-index fat was correct. He had to remind himself to breathe. She crossed to the bed, drew back the covers and lay down, all the while watching him. With a silent apology for how he was feeling, he went to the bed and climbed on next to her. He crooked his arm, put his head in his hand. Still holding her gaze, he ran his fingers down her body, massaged her breasts, leaned over and kissed her rib cage. Then he sat up for access to the back of her knees. Before long she was writhing on the bed. Still, he continued to touch her, surprised that she allowed it.

"I can't get my fill," he uttered before he could censor his words.

"I... Oh, wow, David, right there." Heavy breathing now, but she got out, "Me, either. I feel like it's been forever since we did this."

Somewhere in the recesses of his mind, it registered that they rarely talked during sex, but he was getting so deep into the feel and smell of her, he couldn't think clearly.

A while after that, she tugged him up. They turned on their sides, both of their heads nestled on one of the fluffy


153

pillows, their faces a breath apart. The urge to kiss her was so strong, it almost overcame him. Almost. Instead, he opened her legs and thrust inside her, but still gently, tenderly, lovingly. They came together in a cataclysm of pleasure.

Neither spoke when she cuddled into him.

When he pulled the covers up.

Or when they both closed their eyes. David's last thought was they hadn't kissed, but they'd both broken the rules of their bargain.

# CHAPTER 11

THE CELEBRATION OF Madison Lansing's birthday was boisterous, and so full of genuine love, it made Alisha miss her friends even more. As she stared at the yard where the double wedding had taken place months ago, she was happy for them all but felt nostalgic for the times when they lived or worked together.

"Penny for your thoughts." Celeste mouthed the crazy idiom when she came up to Alisha. They were all acclimating.

"I was remembering your weddings out here in the backyard." Alisha could still recall the crystalline sky, hot sun and what lovely…brides…they all made.

By Celeste's side, their dog Bruiser waited for her to pet him. Alisha was still amazed at their connection. Celeste said the baby even kicked when he nuzzled her stomach and Bruiser never jumped on Celeste. "I can't wait for fall and winter. Can you imagine snow? The children tell me it's wonderful."

The joy in Celeste's voice brought a grin to Alisha's face. "And after the new year, you'll have another one to spoil."

"That I will." She patted her baby bump, and her eyes misted. "I can't believe it."

Before Alisha could comment, David came up to them. "You're in for a treat, Lisha." He held up a piece of food. "Here, taste this."

"What is it?"

"A beef roll, commonly known as a hot dog. And I have no idea where the name came from."

She took a bite. It was spongy but cooked with something spicy on it. "Is that mustard?"

"Uh-huh. You like?"

"Yes."

"I'll get you one."

She stayed David's arm. "Not now. I had some of that cheese Celi put out."

"Let me know when I can fix it for you." When David left, she realized he seemed tired today, and edgy. Then she noticed the look on Celeste's face. "Why are you gaping at me?"

"Because a man just fed you food."

"Is that not acceptable?"

"Of course it is. It's just intimate."

Geez, why wasn't she more careful? The last thing Alisha wanted was for Celeste and Dorian to know she was sleeping with David.

"You drove down with him, didn't you?"

"Yes, Celi. You know we've become good friends." She tried to sound impatient, to ward off more questions, but David had softened her and the tone came out weak.

"Hmm, seems like more."

"It isn't. Now, let's go find out what games the kids want to play."

Maddy, Jon and Cody were at a picnic table, Maddy taking notes. "Hi, birthday girl," Celeste said, tousling her new daughter's hair. "What did you come up with?"

Looking up at Celeste, Maddy gave her the most loving look she'd ever seen on a teenager's face. "Three-legged races, bocce ball, badminton and croquet, if we feel like one more."

Celeste and Alisha exchanged looks. Maddy noticed. "Don't tell me you don't know how to play any of them, Aunt Alisha."

The first time the kids called her that she'd been shocked. But they still thought the three of them were blood sisters.

"I asked David what we might do here, and when he said play games, he suggested we try badminton. So we had a few games in our backyard."

While the kids went to tell the others their plan, Celeste's eyes narrowed on Alisha. "*Our* backyard?"

"Did I say that?"

"Yes." She reached out, but Alisha stepped back. "Honey, if something's going on between you two, you can share your feelings with me."

A phony smile on her face. "We're buddies. I like him. End of story." She pulled her cell phone out of the pocket of her capris. "Now, let's find out what those other games are."

• • •

DAVID WATCHED ALISHA and Celeste talk with the Lansing kids and sighed heavily. The sun bounced off her hair, which was really lighter now. He was struggling to put up a good front but was finding it hard to pretend. Last week, when they made love at her house (and that's what they'd done), things had shifted for him. Oh, they'd been hot and heavy twice since then in their stranger mode, but they'd forgone the hotel each time and spent the night together in his bed.

Alex approached with two beers and handed one to David. "They're beauties, aren't they?"

"They are." He sipped the cold liquid. "And you're smitten."

Casually, Alex socked David in the arm. "So what are you waiting for? Jump in. The water's fine."

"I'm already drowning." Fuck! He hadn't meant to say that.

"I mean, drowning in, um…"

"You don't have to explain." He stared with adoration at his wife. "Since I first laid eyes on Celeste, I wanted her. I'm thinking you feel the same about Alisha."

"No, you misunderstand; we're friends."

Folding his arms over his chest, he just watched David. "Do you know you touch each other whenever you're in proximity? You rub shoulders, link arms sometimes, and you're always looking to see where the other is."

"Celeste's powers rubbing off on you?"

"Just scientific observations."

"You're wrong, Alex."

"Sure I am."

They had to get off this topic. It would feel too good to confide in someone who knew the whole story. Well, most of it, anyway. "Has your new ethics program gotten off the ground yet?"

They spoke for a few minutes about Alex's courses at a local college, then Alex was dragged away by Cody.

David realized he wasn't covering up his feelings very well. What was between him and Alisha was out of hand, and after he prayed about their relationship, he believed there was only one way to fix it. He had to come clean with her. Tell her he loved her, as a man loves a woman, that he wanted a life with her and ask her to consider going further with him. He knew the risk—perhaps she wouldn't sleep with him again because he'd broken his promise—but he also knew her feelings had changed, too. She was pretending, too. He'd only put the talk off because he didn't want to spoil this gathering that had been planned for weeks.

Maddy blew a whistle and, when everyone gathered around, announced they'd start with a badminton tournament. Two nets had been set up so all the kids could play. Alisha, David, Alex, Dorian and Helen took to the makeshift court. In the first round, David was paired up with Alisha, of course, and by standing behind her, got to appreciate her long legs and nice behind, revealed by the cropped things she wore. The little birdie flew over the net, and Alisha aced it. Cody, in front, on his side, frowned. When it happened a second time, David called out, "Time. I need to confer with my partner."

He moved in close and pulled down the bill of the cap she'd put on to avoid sunburn out here in the hot sun. "Lisha, it's customary to take it easy on the children."

"Earnestly?" Her eyes were wide with surprise.

"Earnestly."

"Even Maddy?"

"They're kids."

"When I was her age, I wouldn't have wanted anyone to let me win at a contest."

A chuckle escaped him even though his heart hurt at the thought of losing her. "No, of course you wouldn't."

The rest of the game went better, but David and Alisha still won that game and the three that followed. After the last, Luke called out, "Congrats, guys."

When they were leaving the court, he couldn't resist a pat on Alisha's ass.

"David!" she warned.

"Common practice in sports for the winners."

"I can't believe it."

"It is, darlin'" Leaning in closer he whispered, "Roll with the punches."

He left her to get his beer, laughing at her confused expression.

• • •

ALISHA WAS SHOCKED at David's playfulness. Right here in front of everybody. Okay, she knew things had changed between them, but she was hoping it was only temporary. The night they'd eaten the lasagna, they'd been different with each other. She'd wanted him to kiss her. She'd wanted *intimacy*. But that was the only time she'd felt uncomfortable with her reaction to him. The next two times were purely physical, though they took place in one of their beds. But today, they were acting like a couple. Which wasn't good. It was just she missed everybody who was here so much, she didn't want to admonish him, she didn't want to be in a bad mood. She just wanted to have fun. So she let herself go.

And won at croquet.

Her team came in first at bocce.

Her friends teased her on a break in the play about being driven. She accepted it with good humor.

Then the time came for the three-legged races. She was determined not to compete with David, so she asked to assign the partners. She picked Dorian as hers and paired David up with Cody.

Dorian interrupted her announcement of the teams. "I, um, can't do that race." Her face was…flushed and her eyes wide with pleasure.

The group turned to look at her.

Luke stood next to her, his arm hooked around her neck in that affectionate way of his. "Celi and Helen are bowing out because we usually fall all over the place with these races. Dorian's bowing out, too."

Quiet. Then Cody asked, "What does he mean, Dad?"

Maddy answered. "She's like them. She's gonna have a baby."

Everyone rushed to Dorian but Alisha. For some reason, the news made her sad. So she slipped out of the group and walked around the house to the front to collect her feelings. David found her sitting on the steps of the porch before she had time to reason out her reaction. "Hey, are you okay?"

She stared at the street of this lovely neighborhood. The grass was really green, a breeze blew through the trees and the flowers were still in bloom. "I'm having some negative reaction to Dorian's news. I didn't want her to see it."

Dropping down on the concrete step, he sat close to her. A car drove by slowly, as there were a lot of children living here. "Negative? How? Why?"

"I don't exactly know."

He waited a long time to ask, "Don't you?"

"No. But obviously, you do." Her tone was snapping. "What do you think?"

"That you feel left out, for one thing." He brushed her hair off her check in a tender gesture. "Both her and Celi are pregnant, as is Helen."

"I'm happy for them, David. How can you believe otherwise after what happened with our society and what we had to do to fix it?"

"That's not what I meant. All right, I'm going to ask this. Do you want all that for yourself?"

"What?"

"A child. A family." He rubbed his hand on her knee. "A husband." The last was husky. Hoarse. Caring.

"I've told you many times, I don't."

"You can change your mind. About any of it."

"Of course I can. But I don't want to." Without saying more, she stood, and when she started back to the group, she thought she heard him mumble, "Liar."

But she refused to think about his questions.

• • •

LATER THAT NIGHT, David was feeling the stress of the day, of the week, hell, maybe of the last few months. Since the Sisters of Doom had arrived, his life had been turned upside down. They'd all settled in the backyard, with the crickets chirping as background music. Alex and the kids had made a bonfire, which blazed brightly and fascinated Celeste, Dorian and Alisha. The scent of roasting marshmallows permeated the air as the Lansings' kids stuck sticks of them into the fire.

Celeste and Alex took up space in one chaise, Dorian and Luke in another, and Jess and Helen were seated next to each other, holding hands. Alisha stayed on the other side of the yard, cuddling Bruiser, who'd taken a liking to her. David sipped his coffee and stared up at the sky. Squeals came from the children—the younglings—a murmur of voices filtered through the group and slowly his eyes closed.

"David, wake up." Alisha's sexy voice. He felt weight on the chaise and reached for her. "David, you fell asleep. The others are ready to go inside."

He rubbed his eyes. "Asleep? For how long?"

"An hour. You're exhausted with all you do for others."

"I'm fine. I didn't mean to miss the party."

Someone must have taken his coffee out of his hand and put it on the table. "You should have awakened me."

"No one could bear to. I'm going up, too."

"Ah." He held her gaze. "Where am I sleeping?"

"The leather couch in Alex's office pulls out to a bed. The kids are on the third floor and the rest of us are taking the children's rooms. I have Cody's."

"Why don't you sleep with me?" The words rolled off his tongue before he could stop them, but by now, the backyard was empty of listeners and his defenses had lowered because of his nap.

"I can't. You know that."

"But you want to?"

"Yes. I'd like to join. I've been thinking about it all day."

"Hmm."

She stood, back-dropped by the glow of the embers. "I'm going in."

"Fine. I'll just stay out here a little while longer."

"Good night, then."

When he was alone, he closed his eyes again but not to sleep.

*So, is this how it's going to be?*

He waited for God to answer.

*"Yeah, I guess. I shouldn't have asked for more. I'm sorry."*

Once he had God's forgiveness for going back on his agreement, for pushing Alisha when he promised not to, he rose and made his way into the house. The interior was dim, still and quiet. He found the den and opened the door. Through the moonlight, he could see the bed had been pulled out and made up.

He also saw a silhouette seated, facing him. He gasped.

It was Alisha.

• • •

163

SHE SAT STILL as stone. David had stopped abruptly, stared over at her but didn't speak. Was he was as surprised to see her as she was to have come down here? She'd gotten to Cody's room, with its cute little toys all around and his bed like a car, undressed and slipped under the covers. But she was unable to sleep. Her body yearned for David, but her mind, her soul yearned for him, too. She'd risen and watched through the window facing the back where David had been sitting when she left him. He was praying. She knew it. She couldn't articulate what had driven her to wait for him, but she'd been compelled to come to his sleeping room.

He said from the doorway, "Why are you here, Alisha?"

"I want to be with you. Lock the door."

"No."

Her heart rate sped up. "Why?"

"I won't break my promise to you again. I made vows to God."

"Come here, David." She patted the side of the mattress. "Let's talk."

Turning, he snicked the lock. "All right, we'll talk and I don't want to be interrupted. But then you have to leave. Promise me."

"I promise I'll leave if you want me to after we discuss things."

His steps were heavy as he crossed to her. His shoulders sagged. His weariness was partly caused by her. When he reached the bed, he sat down next to her and took her hand. "I can't do this anymore, love."

He'd never called her that. She'd told herself she didn't want the word, the concept, but her heart soared when he uttered it.

"What can't you do?"

"I can't join with you."

She'd never expected that. "Oh." She started to rise, but he held her back.

"I want to make love to you. I know I said our physical relationship would never go down that road, but it has. It happened last Saturday night. I couldn't help myself. But I won't pretend anymore."

She waited, thinking about him, about their relationship, about her friends and what they'd risked. Finally, she said, "Then kiss me."

• • •

THEIR MOUTHS MET, mated, melded together. It was so much more intense than the time David was teaching her, he almost couldn't tolerate the sensations that shot through him like wildfire spreading out of control. Angling his head, he probed her lips, and she opened to him like the sweetest of flowers. Her hand cupped his neck, held him close, and she exerted her own pressure with her lips. His mind went berserk at her participation, at her attempt to devour him, encouraging him to consume her. Taking her with him, he laid back on the bed, their mouths still connected. She stretched out on the mattress and moved so their bodies aligned. He took it further, bracing himself over her so their chests were flush. Her curves felt so good against him, her body yielding and demanding at the same time. They re-angled their heads and the kiss went on. When that wasn't enough, his hand found her breast and massaged her. The moan that escaped her was low and throaty, driving him further under her spell. He opened the robe she wore and found her nipple with his mouth. Her body lurched. Never had any connection been so meaningful.

She whispered, "Clothes. Off."

He freed her from her robe. She tore at the buttons of his shirt, pulled it off his shoulders and made quick work of his pants and briefs. Their naked bodies aligned from mouth to foot as they kissed again. Her hands roamed over his back, his neck, in his hair. Nothing he hadn't done before, but so different, in so many ways. His mind blanked as she allowed him to do the same with her, explore her with the utmost gentleness.

It wasn't enough and he wondered if it ever would be.

"I want to be inside you," he said hoarsely.

"I want that, too."

He managed a sitting position, then he knelt, leaned back and drew her up. She straddled him, opened to him as he eased her down on his penis. Their chests came together. She buried her face in his neck and he did the same in hers. His thrusts were gentle at first. They became faster, harder, but never did they lose their tenderness.

When it was time, they spiraled together, in a burst of such sweet pleasure that tears formed in David's eyes. She called out his name, he whispered hers, and then he ceased to think at all.

When they came back to consciousness, they were still wrapped around each other. David felt the cool air on his hot skin and she shivered. "Lie down, and let's cover up."

She did so, without speaking. They cuddled together under the blanket and were silent for a long time. Finally, he opened his mouth to speak, just as his phone buzzed. Damn it.

"I'm sorry, I have to get that. People I know are in pain, and I might be needed."

"Go ahead. I understand."

Fishing for his phone from his pants, which were still on the bed, he clicked into it. "David Ryan."

"David, this is Brian Young."

His heartbeat escalated. "Brian. What's wrong?"

"Hal Hanson's church was hit again. It's all over the news."

"Hit, as in arson? Somebody set the church on fire this time?"

"And burned it to the ground."

"Oh, Dear Lord. Is Hal hurt?"

"Badly. I went to the hospital with my collar on so I could get in to see him. He's burned. And he hasn't regained consciousness. I think you should come over."

"Brian, I'm in Virginia. But I'll drive back. It'll take a while, though."

"Just hurry. I don't know how long he'll be…"

"Keep the faith, Brian. See you soon."

He hadn't noticed that Alisha had gotten out of bed and was dressed in the robe again. "Hal Hanson?" He nodded.

"And it's bad?"

"Yes."

"I'm going upstairs to dress. Then we better get going."

"We? Honey, you don't have to come with me. Stay and enjoy tomorrow with your friends."

"No. Pack your things. I'll grab mine and leave a note. No need to wake the others in the middle of the night."

He nodded. But didn't move. This wasn't going to end well. He just knew it. Leaning over, she kissed his lips briefly. "Up, and hurry David. We have to go."

• • •

"2 THESSALONIANS 1:7-9 And to you who are troubled rest with us, when the Lord Jesus shall be revealed from heaven with his mighty angels, in flaming fire taking vengeance on them that know not God, and that obey not the gospel of our Lord Jesus Christ: Who shall be punished with everlasting destruction from the presence of the Lord, and from the glory of his power;

Your loyal Servant, always."

# CHAPTER 12

ALISHA SAT IN the chapel at Memorial Hospital, where they'd waited for news of Helen's pregnancy, what seemed like a lifetime ago. David had brought her directly here and said it would be a comfort to him to have her with God.

She stared at the beautifully carved, smooth, pews — ten of them — the polished floor and altar table made of wood. A real god wouldn't want people of today to waste his resources.

Turning her attention away from her surroundings, she thought about the fire. Poor Hal. And poor David. He'd been silent on the drive from Virginia to New York. For a while, she'd tried to get him to talk, then she just gave up and put her hand on his knee. From time to time, he'd cover it with his, but he didn't speak. She knew he believed Hal was going to die. When he'd asked her to wait here, she hadn't the heart to deny him.

She stared at the altar accusingly. *Where the hellor are you now, David's god? That man, men like him, men like Hal have dedicated their lives to you and you let this happen? What kind of deity are you?*

David would be sad that she was chiding his god. But it made her feel better. She closed her eyes and leaned back against the pew.

*I'm the kind of deity that has given man free will, Alisha, my child. And evil comes out of that freedom. But so does good.*

Her eyes snapped open and she jerked forward. Looked around. No one was here. Everything looked the same. Still, her heart thrust against her chest. What had just happened? Think, Lisha, think logically. You were scolding god for this atrocity, and all right, other evil things in the world, and you simply filled in a response. That's all it was. With a heavy sigh, she settled back.

*That's not the way it works.*

No, no, it couldn't be. She had to be going into some altered psychological state she'd read about in her research on religion. Where people saw visions, induced stigmata on their hands and feet, believed, actually *believed* God talked to them.

*I do. On occasion. And you, young lady, need my direct attention. I thought engineering your relationship with David would be enough. But obviously not.*

She buried her face in her hands. How could this be happening?

David found her that way and asked solicitously, "Sweetheart, are you okay?"

Stunned, she looked up at him.

"What's wrong? You're white and trembling. Do you hurt somewhere?"

She could only shake her head. He took her hands. Fear made them cold. She was quivering inside.

"Alisha," he said more firmly. "What happened? Why are you so upset?"

Standing, she threw herself into his arms. "Oh, David, your…your…your god talked to me."

His whole body relaxed. "Well, it's about time."

• • •

"HERE, DRINK THIS. I'd give you a shot of whiskey if I could get some here, but this is probably better for you."

"What is it?" she asked. Even Alisha's voice quavered.

"The tea you like so much. It'll soothe you."

"I'm fine."

"You are not fine." David sat down and watched her. "You're probably in shock."

"I am not. I simply had a hallucination."

He managed a chuckle. It was wrong to be feeling such joy when his friend was dying upstairs, but he couldn't express how happy he was about what had occurred in that little chapel. He'd brought her to the cafeteria to talk. "You aren't hallucinating. God reached out to you." David knew that in his bones.

"David, no. It's this god talk you spout all the time. And our disagreements about religion. Everything finally got to me because I'm so worried about you." She frowned. "And because of what happened last night."

Incredible warmth swelled inside him. "We're going to table what happened last night for a while."

She ran her fingers over the wood surface of where they sat.

He touched her hand. "It means to postpone something. We'll discuss last night later."

Nodding, she sipped the tea and studied him. "Why did you come down from Hal's room? Is there news?"

"Jeb and Brian, my minister friends, are in with Hal."

Reaching out, she turned her hand to clasp his. "How is he?"

David's heart ached as it had in the war. "He's going to die, Alisha. He's burned over eighty percent of his body."

"I'm sorry."

He drew in a heavy breath. "We have to catch this maniac. He's killing my friends."

"I'm sorry," she reiterated.

He spoke what was in his mind and soul. "You could stop this, Alisha."

"What?"

"You can find out who the arsonist is with the click of a few buttons."

She stilled. And closed down. He'd seen it enough before they'd gotten close, and he was sorry to have done this to her. But God had sent her to him for a reason. He knew that now. So he waited. There was a buzz of conversation from other patrons in the large room, and the smell of pizza and cooked meat. David took her silence until she decided to answer him.

"You know I can't do that."

"I know you don't want to. But you have the means. Alisha, my friend is going to die. Who will be next?"

"David, no." Her voice was tortured. "I can't find out who's doing this. What if it alters the future?"

"You've already changed the future twice."

"Which is my point. We can't risk changing something back, or in a way that will hurt my people."

*"We're* your people now."

"No. The Guardians instructed us not to tamper with anything else."

"This is saving lives, honey."

"No."

He sat back. He shouldn't be pushing her, because she was in such bad shape already. And, in truth, he didn't really know if he was right.

He was about to back off when Joe Destino came to their table. Lines of worry and fatigue marred his brow. "David?"

"Joe? What are you doing here?"

The man stared at his and Alisha's clasped hands on the table. She withdrew hers. "I came over to see how the reverend was. The situation doesn't look good."

David shook his head. "No, it doesn't."

"But I have some other news. I just got a call from the police. They think they've caught the arsonist."

Briefly, David glanced at Alisha. "Lord in heaven, who is it?"

"A friend of yours. Jase Carpenter."

David's jaw dropped. "Jase? No, he's only a kid."

"Most arson is committed by youth. They found him wandering around the crime scene. I'm headed to the police station now, but I thought you might want to come with me to talk to him."

David closed his eyes against this reality. *No, no, please God. Not this.*

"I can't believe it's him. He's so gentle."

Then he remembered Jase called the group *hooligans*. David had suspected he was eavesdropping the night Ken Evans used the term in relation to the boys. They'd been discussing the arson with Joe. No, no, he still couldn't believe Jase was capable of cold-blooded killing.

"Apparently," Joe continued, "there's circumstantial evidence. The police checked his file. He's been arrested for setting a couple of minor fires before, and his parents bought their way out of the incidents. But now, mom and dad kicked him out of the house a few days ago."

"What?"

"He let it slip to the police that they made him leave because he's gay—and their religion is totally homophobic." He cocked his head. "Religion, David. Churches have been hit."

"But that doesn't mean—"

Impatient now, Joe checked his watch. "Look, I'm here because we're friends and I thought you might be able to help. But I've got to go interview him. If you don't want to come with me, it's your choice."

David stood quickly. "I'll come with you, but you're wrong." He glanced over at Alisha, who'd said nothing. "Would you like to come?"

She shook her head.

Fishing his keys out of his pocket, he set them on the table. "Go home, then. I'll have Joe drop me there when we're done."

She nodded. Torn between staying with her when she was in such a vulnerable state, angry that she refused to end this curse on all of them, he said simply, "I'll see you later," and left the cafeteria with Joe.

• • •

ALISHA SETTLED WITH Dorian in the living room of her half of the duplex, on the almost-conforming couch she'd helped choose and gave her friend a weak smile. "I can't believe you came back to New York early."

"I'm concerned about you, and Luke wanted to be here for David. Jess and Helen did, too." Dorian studied her. At least, she couldn't touch Alisha and know her feelings. Hellor, Alisha didn't even know what they were.

After catching up on what had happened with Hal Hanson, and now Jase Carpenter, Dorian took a sip of her ice water and lazed back on the cushions. "Now that's over, I want to know what else is happening with you and David." When Alisha started to object, Dorian held up her hand. "No, don't try to put me off like you did Celi. We know your relationship with David has changed. It was obvious to all of us when we were in Virginia. But maybe you don't see it. Sometimes when you're in the frame, you can't see the whole picture."

Alisha had to smile at the idiom. "Show-off."

But Dorian was right. The others would have picked up on the way she and David reacted to each other. In any case, what was inside her was about to explode, so she needed to release her frustration. "Things have changed, probably more than you realize."

"Then tell me."

"We've been joining for several weeks."

"I knew it. You're both more relaxed."

"I wouldn't say that. Not now, especially." Not after last night. "But the sex was wonderful."

"Was? Aren't you joining anymore?"

Alisha swallowed hard. "No."

"Why?"

"Because last night, in Celi's den, we made love."

"Hallelujah!" Dorian jumped off her couch, hugged Alisha awkwardly, then sat back down.

"It happened without our consent, as did the whole journey up to this. He hadn't even kissed me until then. Well, except for... Never mind."

Dorian got a dreamy expression on her face. "Isn't kissing great?"

"Yes, it was perfect."

"Then why do you look like you're going to cry?"

"Because there's a real problem between us." She ran a restless hand through her hair. "Damn it, Dorian, this is why I didn't want to get involved emotionally with him."

"Honey, you've been involved emotionally with David for months. You've simply taken it to another level. Is it that bad?"

"I wish I didn't care for him so much."

"Why?"

"Because he asked me to do something for him, and it's wrong, but I want to do it anyway. I've lost my ability to think clearly and logically when a situation concerns him."

Dorian's hand went to her mouth. "Oh, Lisha, David wouldn't lure you into a relationship just to get something from you. He isn't that kind of man."

Alisha froze with her wine glass halfway to her mouth. "I hadn't thought he was. Until you said that. Oh, no, Dorian, what if that's really why he brought me into this relationship?"

"It isn't. I know him. He'd never do that."

She knew him, too, knew he wouldn't act so unethically, but still, the thought took hold in her brain.

"What did he ask of you?"

Her heart ached for how he was suffering. "His friend was hurt last night."

"So you said. If David wants you to help him, it's a moot point. The Multimed can't prevent death."

"What? Oh, no, that isn't what he wants. He asked me to use the computeller to find out who's setting the fires at churches."

"Oh." Her dark brows furrowed. "We agreed not to use the computellers to change anything else."

"I'm thinking of confiscating them."

"Maybe that would be wise. We don't want to alter the good we've done. The tasks we finally managed to complete."

Slowly, Alisha set her glass down, the wine tasting sour, like everything else today. "And finding the arsonist prematurely would certainly alter history."

Dorian blew out a heavy breath. "This is a true dilemma. I can see David's side of it. All his friends are being hurt by some...torch, Luke calls them."

"I'm conflicted because I want to help David." She wasn't going to tell Dorian about her other conflict. With his god.

Thoughtful, Dorian stared out the front window, to where the leaves swayed in the breeze. Suddenly, her eyes widened and her mouth dropped.

Alisha glanced toward the window but didn't see anything. "What's wrong?"

"Oh, no, Lisha, I just thought of something. Something awful."

"Tell me."

"What if you don't use the computeller, and there's another fire?" She waited, her eyes bleak. "And David is hurt? Or worse?"

• • •

DAVID SAT ACROSS from Jase at a steel table in the police-interrogation room, which smelled like sweat and was cold. The boy's slim shoulders slumped, his eyes were grim and his mouth tight. Joe Destino was present because they wouldn't let David see Jase alone.

"Talk to me, son." David kept his voice calm and soothing. "I can help."

Jase eyed Joe. "He a cop?"

Arson investigators were law enforcement officials, too. "Yes. Primarily, he's the arson investigator."

"Then I'm not talkin'."

From across the table, David gently put a hand on Jase's arm. "You know that only makes you look guilty."

"Mince says we all look guilty because the cops think we're troublemakers."

"That's not true. But you're *in* trouble, and you need to help clear yourself. Did you call your parents?"

"The 'rents kicked me out."

"They told the police it was because you're gay."

His eyes slipped to Joe again. "Don't want to talk about that, either."

"Maybe not now. But when this is all over, we'll discuss how you're feeling about that. I've had a lot of experience with the LGBTQ community. I can help you deal with coming out."

Looking older now, the boy rolled his eyes. "Nobody can help me."

"Is that why you torched the churches?" Joe Destino asked.

"I didn't torch any churches."

"Don't you hate religion after what your parents did to you?"

David asked, "Jase, did you ask for a lawyer?"

"Why?"

"If you've requested one, Captain Destino can't question you until he gets here."

Joe's face reddened. "Hell, David—"

David slapped his hand on the table, its sound tinny in the small room. "The boy has rights, Joe. We can't violate them."

Jase's face contorted. "Tell that to my parents."

"Ask for a lawyer, Jase."

"No." The boy shook his head. "They'll have to pay him, and I don't want anything from them ever again."

"The court will appoint one then, Jase."

"No."

Hunching forward, on the same side of the table as David, Joe asked, "So, why were you at the church?"

Instead of directing his answer to Joe, Jase talked to David. "You were away, Rev."

"What?"

"You told us last time we played ball you were bookin' to Virginia this weekend."

"I did." Ah, he understood now. "And because you couldn't get me you went to another church?"

"No, I went to see Reverend Hal."

"I didn't know you were that close to him."

"He was at the picnic for the refugees. I talked to him and that other guy, Reverend Brian. We were shootin' the shit and they told me they liked" — the boy's eyes teared; one renegade drop slipped down his cheeks — "what you were doing with us. Reverend Hal told me you taught him some stuff this time."

David swallowed hard. "Hal was my mentor when I first came to New York."

"He was proud of you. And he said if me or any of the other kids couldn't get in touch with you, to call him."

Destino asked, "Why'd you go see him Saturday night?"

"I was feelin'... I was feelin'..." Then Jase clammed up.

David had seen the same look on the kid's face on young men with battle fatigue. Men who were about to give up.

But he waited to see what Jase would do. The boy put his head down on the table and mumbled something.

"What was that, Jase?" David asked.

Looking up, the boy quietly told him he was suicidal.

• • •

ALISHA WATCHED FROM the front porch as David pulled into his driveway. He hadn't been home all night but had called to tell her he'd gone back to the hospital. When she asked about Jase Carpenter and the arrest, he said Jase had been released because the only things the police had against him were he was at the church and circumstantial evidence. Since he was a juvenile, they couldn't hold him more than eight hours without pressing formal charges. David also said he would be at the hospital indefinitely.

And Alisha knew that meant until Hal Hanson died.

Dorian's words plagued her. *David could get hurt. Or worse.* David could die.

His face was grim as he came up the walk. And he didn't speak to her. He simply held out his hand to take hers, unlocked his door, and led her inside. Once in the foyer, fat tears fell onto his cheeks. "He's dead, Lisha. My friend is dead."

She reached for him and he practically fell into her arms. Though he was taller, he held on to her like a lifeline. She grasped him tightly. He really let go then. Deep, wrenching sobs tore out of him. She said only, "I'm so sorry."

Would he say, *You could have prevented it?* Should he say that to her?

He didn't. He just cried. When he calmed, he moved back, pulled a cloth piece out of his pocket and blew his nose. "Wow, I can't remember the last time I did that. If ever."

"You were entitled." She held on to his hand and led him to the leather couch. Once they were seated, she cuddled into him. "Tell me what happened."

"He never regained consciousness. Thank God. He'd have been in agony. The three of us, Brian, Jeb and I were by his side. It appeared to be an easy passing."

"Do you believe he's with your god? If so, that makes it better."

"Not corporeally. Not even mentally. Mostly, I believe our souls join with God's when we pass. I do believe there's a deeper connection with God then."

She didn't respond. It was a nice idea, if erroneous. They talked about holding services for Hal. Funerals weren't held in her time, but she knew of the custom. "One of the deacons in his church said Hal had written a document that he'd like me to do his funeral if he died first. And it was odd — Jeb was with me when the deacon relayed the information, and he seemed shocked. I didn't know he and Hal had become friends, but he said Hal was helping him look for full time pastorship."

"Will you hold the ritual?"

"Yes." He hugged her close. "Will you come?"

"If you want me to."

"You'd actually come to church?" he asked.

"For you, I would. If it would comfort you."

He sighed. "We have to talk. About more than one thing."

"Not when you haven't had any sleep. Or are this emotionally drained. But later, yes. When I get back from my job interview with the Museum this afternoon, we can talk."

"I'd forgotten it was today." He clasped her to him. "Come to bed with me?"

"Of course."

"To sleep. I'm afraid I'm not up, so to speak, for anything else."

She chuckled. "I'd love to lie next to you. Hold you. I didn't get much rest last night, either."

Together, they made their way to his bedroom. It was so different from hers, with a lake of a bed, masculine tones of brown and black on the quilt and chairs, and dark wood furniture. They undressed, slid under the covers and settled on a pillow. In minutes, David was asleep.

But as she held him, her mind whirled. If she'd done what he asked of her, his friend would be alive. If she'd done what he asked of her, David wouldn't be so despondent. But worse than even that horrible thought was the undeniable fact that David wasn't safe. The arsonist hadn't been caught. Would David and his church be the next target?

# CHAPTER 13

DAVID AWOKE. IMMEDIATELY, one thought claimed him—Hal was dead. A wave of sadness swamped him, so deep it crippled his insides. He buried his head in the pillow and prayed for strength. For tolerance of this awful emotion. After a good five minutes, he felt as if he could cope. But he still didn't get up. Turning over, he realized that Alisha had gone to her interview. For a job. At the museum. When they discussed the work, as if it was created just for her, she'd said, I'm thinking *of one of the theories of time travel—that if people go back to the past and change it, that they were meant all along to be here and alter the present.*

Linking his hands behind his head, he stared up at the ceiling fan, listening to its soft whir. But she'd also stated definitively, *Our interference must stop with Alex, with our last task, assigned by the Guardians*

And then just recently, after Hal was hurt.

*You know I can't do that,* she'd said of his second request.

*I know you don't want to. But you have the means. Alisha, my friend is going to die. Who will be next?*

There were so many ramifications of her stance. The most significant of them was could he ever forgive her if another of the clergy died? And could she ever forgive herself if he did?

• • •

THE MUSEUM OF Anthropological Studies in Manhattan stood six stories tall amidst the other buildings in the city. Its stone front was etched with a variety of ancient symbols and was as impressive as this huge office she now sat in, across from Damien Riggs. "Thanks for coming today. Sorry we couldn't get you in sooner."

"It wasn't that long. I appreciate the opportunity." This interviewing business was complicated. Luke had told her to be deferent, something that didn't come easy to her. And she was having a hellor of a time keeping David out of her mind—she could still hear his wrenching sobs.

Riggs picked up his tablet and scrolled down on it. "Your résumé is detailed and impressive, if I may be frank."

"Again, thank you."

"Undergrad in anthropology, MA in behavioral studies at Yale and a PhD from Carnegie Mellon. Top schools, top grades."

"Studying the future in relation to the past has been the focus for my entire professional life."

"Yes, your previous employers mentioned that. As do the letters of reference." Jess, Luke, and Helen had been given pseudonyms and fictionalized backgrounds on the Internet using the computeller. "But I'd like to hear from you why you concentrate on the future."

Her chin raised. "Mr. Riggs, the world is in danger. I know that as much as I know my own name. What we're doing today to our environment and the advances in medicine can bring about a world of untold consequences."

"Elaborate on that notion."

To keep her hands from fisting, she grasped the chair arms. This wasn't a *notion*. "With the explosion of technology, future generations will see cyber wars that could unleash horrible chemical and biological weapons."

"I happen to agree with you. We have evidence of sarin gas and nuclear armament now. What do you think the effect of those weapons will be?"

"The near destruction of humankind. And the planet."

He folded his arms across his chest. Backdropped by Manhattan, he seemed...powerful. "Isn't that a bit dramatic?"

She had to calm herself down before she responded. "I'm sorry; I feel very passionate about this."

A smile. "So I see. I like that."

"Perhaps we should discuss each of the projects I would oversee if I were to take this position."

Something flickered across his face. "Are you interviewing for other jobs?"

Luke had coached her on this, too. "Yes. I've had five meetings with other institutions."

"Then by all means, give me your thoughts on our projects. Looks like we'll have to act quickly if we're to snag you."

*Thank you, Luke.*

She pulled out her own smart phone (a total misnomer). "I've listed them all, but I have the most comments on the first five. May we start with the effects of oil spills on the continents?" Eventually, oil was outlawed as a source of energy but not before a huge pipeline destroyed the countryside of half of the United Americans, Canada. The same spill irrevocably polluted the Atlantic Ocean.

She had to think hard, though, about how to convey the information as conjecture, not fact. Even if it had come true.

The interview lasted until six o'clock, at which time they asked to take her to dinner. It was the last thing she wanted to do. She *wanted* to get home to David, to see how he was, to comfort him, but she smiled and said, "How lovely."

• • •

MUCH AS HE'D done that night almost six weeks ago, David called all the area ministers together at his church. They sat in the fellowship hall, as they had then, around small tables. He'd opened the windows and the rich smell of almost fall settled around them.

"Thanks for coming everybody." David stood in front of the group. "I'd like to start this out by honoring Hal. If you'll all bow your heads."

He gave a prayer asking for Hal's soul to be joyous in its new home, by asking God to help all of them gathered here to cope with their sorrow and asking for guidance, too.

Then the comments began.

"What are we going to do about this maniac? Any of us could be next." This from Kerry Mackenzie. "Even I'm not safe, after he hit my church. Hal's was targeted twice."

Brian Young shook his head. "Maybe I'm lucky mine closed. The thought of any of those people being hurt, killed… I don't know how I'd handle that."

"None of us knows that, Brian," David interjected. "We're all trying to muddle through this horrible thing."

"I have a question." Ken Banks spoke commandingly. Bullies often did that, David thought uncharitably. "What happened with that boy, Jase Carpenter? I heard they arrested him and let him go. Seems to me they had their killer."

"Jase is not a killer." David struggled to keep his temper by walking a few paces. "He doesn't have it in him."

"Well, you'd know, David," another female pastor named Shawna commented. "Besides, I don't think it's our job to come here and speculate who the arsonist is. We need to dis-cuss—again—ways to keep us all safe." Joe had mentioned some in their first meeting, but David didn't know what else to do, so this get-together seemed like a good starting place.

Just then, Jeb Morse rushed into the meeting. His hair was askew, his clothes wrinkled and he carried his briefcase. "Sorry I'm late." David had wondered why Jeb hadn't shown up. Brian hadn't known where he was. "But I've got some-thing helpful." Quickly, he went to the front. "Can you pull down the screen against the wall so I can use my computer?"

"Yes, of course. Why, though?"

"My cousin heard about the arsons here. He's a pastor in Canada. They had a spate of fires in his town, too, and they set up what is now a nationally known program for arsons in places of worship."

After David lowered the screen, Jeb faced them. "As I said, this is a prevention program geared specifically for churches." The computer booted up with its familiar ping, and when David connected it to the screen projector, the light came on. "I'll show you. The people who developed this explain it bet-ter than I can."

The presentation was in document form, so Jeb summa-rized some of it and let the group read along the list.

"The first part of this talks about how people feel when their places of worship are hit. The congregation views it as an attack on their values and belief system." He paused. "I agree with this."

Mumbles of assent.

"There are three factors that need to be addressed: exter-nal security, internal security, and community awareness."

He paused. "Let's read them all silently."

When people finished, a Catholic priest asked, "Can we talk about the viability of these actions? For instance, we can't all afford to repaint our churches to stand out more against the landscape. And I heartily object to fencing around churches. It sends the wrong message."

Jeb frowned. "I don't think the project is suggesting we should do every single one. But we might be able to effect some changes."

"There are several that are easy to implement," Kerry put in. "We can illuminate the exterior and entrances better, use motion-activated lighting near doors and windows and keep shrubbery and trees trimmed so the building is easily observable by passing patrols."

"I already do those things at my church." This from a Baptist minister who David respected.

"Well, good," Jeb said.

"But my church sign blocks the building," the same man added. "I can have that moved. And I've left a ladder up a time or two when we've been doing repairs."

Ken grumbled and pointed at the screen. "I certainly hope everybody here is smart enough to keep ground-level doors and first-floor windows locked. Especially after all that's happened."

David wondered why he was being so negative and critical.

Kerry said, "I'm guilty of negligence. We know how the arsonist got into the three churches, including mine; he broke or easily jimmied windows. None of them had dead bolts."

Silence.

Ken continued, "I know I can't afford a burglar alarm or a private security firm to patrol the areas. Who can, in this

ANOTHER TIME

day and age with shrinking congregations and loss of congregants' jobs?"

David suggested, "Maybe we can't afford not to."

For a while, they discussed what they could/could not practically implement. David could see he was noncompliant in a couple of areas: though he did have a list of people who had keys to the church, they never changed the locks when one of the keys went missing. And he doubted he would ever enlist members to profile the congregation — the presentation put it more tactfully — for those who might be dangerous.

It took another hour to discuss community involvement, but when they were done, David felt better. Until one pastor said, "Uh-oh. We missed something. I'm afraid I'm guilty of it." He scanned the group. "Vandalism often precedes the arson attack."

"Hal's church was vandalized," Brian put in.

"So was mine," Kerry admitted.

And David's church had been hit by vandals, too. Twice, in the last year.

• • •

AFTER HER LONG day of being on stage, including a tedious dinner where she had to carefully choose every word she said, Alisha's shoulders, neck and head ached. But still she waited for the knock that came around eleven at night. She rushed to the door, whipped it open and found David, looking equally fatigued. "Hi."

"Hi. I know it's late…"

"I've been waiting for you. Come on in."

"It's warm enough to sit on the patio. There's a nice breeze and I haven't been outside all day."

189

After she got them wine and lit a candle on the little table between them, they settled on the patio chairs. She took his hand. "Was today bad?"

"Meeting with Hal's family was heartbreaking. But it wasn't a bad night."

"What happened tonight?"

He explained about the presentation he'd seen.

She took comfort in the story, except when he noted the vandalism. "Then I fear for you."

"I guess I do, too." Their gazes held, each of them visible above the light from the candle. "I could be next, Lisha." His voice was raw.

"I know."

"Or one of my friends."

No response. Then, "Are you going to ask me again to check the computeller?"

"You know I want you to do it for me and the other pastors."

Suddenly, she remembered the beginning of her conversation with Dorian, and realized it had been in the back of her mind this whole time…

*Oh, Lisha, David wouldn't lure your into a relationship just to get something from you. He isn't that kind of man."*

*"I hadn't thought he was. Until you said that. Oh, no, Dorian, what if that's really why he brought me into this relationship?"*

So she blurted out, "I didn't piece it together before this, but is that what Saturday night at Celeste's was all about?"

His brows furrowed. "I don't understand."

"Did you *make love* to me to tie me emotionally to you so I'd do what you want?"

*"What?"*

"You heard what I said."

"I did, but I can't believe you're asking me that. I can't fathom why you'd *think* that."

"Because it's your people's way. You control through love."

"*I* certainly don't."

She just watched him, distrust making her cold inside. "How do I know that?"

"Because you know the kind of man I am." He stood abruptly. "But obviously, I've been mistaken about you. If you'll excuse me, I've had a long day. I'm going next door."

With that, he turned away from her and walked across the yard to his half of the house.

Alisha just stared after him. She wished she could say hers was just a jerky knee reaction, but it wasn't. Unfortunately, she really did wonder if he'd come to her at Celeste's with that in mind.

*You went to him, Alisha, that night.*

*No, no, not now. I don't need you. I don't want you filling my head.*

She heard no more from David's god. And just like that, she felt terribly alone.

• • •

DAVID SAT IN Hal Hanson's chair on the altar of his church, numb with grief. In the past few days, not only had he lost a man he loved dearly, but he'd ended a relationship with the woman he'd believed he could spend the rest of his life with. He closed his eyes. There was no room here for recriminations. He had to focus on helping Hal's congregation. To release some of his emotions, he let his grief swamp him and poured out his sadness to God as the funeral attendees entered the church.

When it was time to begin the service, he rose, moving slowly, like an old man. "Welcome to a celebration of Hal's life." His voice cracked on the last words and weeping came from around the church. The sanctuary literally pulsed with misery. "Hal left instructions for his funeral, whenever it occurred, and like him, it's progressive in its thinking. He wanted me to talk, he wanted others to speak what was in their hearts, and then" — here he managed a smile — "he left money for a celebration at a local restaurant." David shook his head. "He also left a great deal of his worldly goods" — he nodded to Hal's wife — "...and Ann agrees...to the refugee resettlement program the Brooklyn churches are participating in.

"That was the kind of man Hal was — thoughtful and generous to a fault. I'll never forget when I came to New York after I returned home from Afghanistan. I needed a place to stay in the city while I got my profile together and sought a call. Hal and Ann took me in, shepherded me through the discernment process, and Hal counseled me during the whole first year of my pastorship here at Community Christian."

He went on to tell some funny stories about living with Hal, some poignant ones about Hal sitting up with him when he had nightmares and flashbacks to the war, and of this good man trying to make sense of a world that legally killed each other. Each memory sliced David to his core.

• • •

ALISHA SAT IN the back corner of the church, behind a pillar so David and maybe his god wouldn't see her. She didn't want to distract David or hurt him more with her presence, as they hadn't spoken since their awful conversation outside two nights ago. She'd dreamed about him both nights, but in each dream, they were no longer angry with each other because David was dead.

The notion plagued her as she breathed in the scent of candles lit on the serving table and listened to his anecdotes of the young man David used to be, and about Hal Hanson. Would David die next?

Why, she thought, had she jumped so quickly to the conclusion that he'd used her emotions to get her to find out the identity of the arsonist? Why had she said those awful things to him?

*Because you were afraid, my child.*

Putting her head down on the pew in front of her, she closed her eyes. *Go away, please.*

This wasn't the first time she'd heard his god since that night she'd fought with David. That god had been with her constantly for the last couple of days. She tried to convince herself that god talking to her was only a manifestation of her inner mind. Her unconscious. She was simply saying things to herself.

*Well, fine. I'll start from there. If I'm part of you, a concept I like, then you know what you have to do.*

*No, I can't.*

*Have I steered you wrong so far? You changed the future.*

That was the first time this god told her that. *Have I? Is it better?*

*Yes.*

*So, see? I can't risk anything else.*

*You have free will; you can risk anything you want.*

Alisha closed her eyes tight. *Please stop. My head hurts.*

*All right, I'll stop. For now.*

The service ended with people speaking about Hal and how they loved him, how he'd helped them. How, they wondered, they'd go on without him.

Staring at David, Alisha wondered the same thing about the man she loved.

• • •

DAVID WAS STANDING outside in the bright September day, greeting the attendees before they headed to the restaurant, when he saw Alisha exit the church. So she had come. He remembered their discussion the night Hal died...

*Will you come?*

*If you want me to.*

*You'd actually come to church?*

*For you, I would. If it would comfort you.*

Other than when he'd installed her in the chapel, this was the only time she'd entered a house of worship. His heart soared at the thought at having her here, then plummeted at the memory of what she'd accused him of. Still, he'd be charitable to her. They met halfway across the concrete sidewalk. She wore a demure dress of navy blue, and the slight breeze played havoc with her hair.

She stared up at him with bruised eyes.

"You came. I didn't think you would after how we ended it."

Her eyes moistened. If she started crying—which he'd never seen her do—he wouldn't make it through the next hour. But she battled back the tears. "Is it David? Ended?"

Despite his vow to be kind, her question infuriated him. "How can you think otherwise?"

"I can *hope* otherwise."

That softened him. Reaching out, he touched her arm. "Honey, there's no future for us. Not if you could believe I'd use the most precious thing between us to sway you into doing what you didn't want to do."

He felt a clutch in his heart so strongly, he put his hand over it. "I can't give us another chance. We'll never trust each other." He looked back at the church. "And life is too short. We both deserve happiness that's more...pure."

"David, I-"

Stepping back, he held up his hand. "I have to go. I didn't want to hurt you by ignoring this nice gesture. But we can't be what we were to each other."

"Can we be friends?" she asked a little desperately.

"No." He wouldn't lie. He could never go back to that with her. "I'm sorry. Good-bye."

As he walked away, he wondered if he could survive the loss of her.

*You can, son, if you have to.*

It was hard to take comfort in God's words, but he tried.

# CHAPTER 14

SURROUNDED BY OCCASIONAL pings of the computers, Alisha walked around the brand new lab she'd paid for, allowing the refugee kids to make her smile. There hadn't been much mirth in the last weeks and she'd learned to take pleasure where she could. "Missy Law, come here."

She crossed to a boy named Sigi, who had the biggest brown eyes she'd ever seen. "Look. I know this."

Her smile turned more genuine. She was making progress in teaching the children computer usage. She'd met with the principals of all the schools, and they'd explained what the kids needed to learn to catch up with the others at their grade levels. Compared to her work on traveling to the past, their needs hadn't been hard to implement. And who knew she'd like working with the younglings so much?

Kerry Mackenzie came to the doorway. Ironically, she and Alisha had become friends over the last few weeks. Alisha didn't know, and didn't ask, if she was dating David. But Kerry, perceptive and innately kind, had seen her misery and been sympathetic, even when Alisha refused to talk about what was bothering her.

Now Kerry asked, "May I speak with you, Alisha?"

The kids all turned and greeted Missy Kerry.

Alisha approached her. "Hi. What can I do for you?"

"I have some good news. At least, I hope you'll consider it good. We've gotten money from the Kiwanis, a nationwide humanitarian group, to create some paid positions at the Center. We'd like to offer you one — working directly with the children."

Alisha sighed. "Kerry, I got a job offer from the Museum of Anthropology to supervise a whole host of projects I'm interested in. If I take that position, I'm not sure I can even help out here anymore. I would train a replacement, though."

The woman's eyes reflected genuine disappointment. "I'm sorry to hear that. I think you're wonderful with the students."

*Because I know what it's like to be a stranger in a strange land.*

Kerry's hazel eyes narrowed. "Have you accepted the museum job?"

Edgy, she toyed with the hem of her blouse. "Not yet. I asked for some time to consider their offer. They think I have other job opportunities, but I don't."

"Now you do." She reached out and squeezed Alisha's arm. "At least, think about it. Maybe there's a reason you didn't agree to take the other one right away. God works in mysterious ways."

"So I've heard."

The petite woman, who was prettier to Alisha these days, started to step away but stopped. "Have you seen David lately? He hasn't answered any of my calls, nor come to the Center to volunteer. I'm worried about his depression over Hal."

"Um, no. I haven't seen him." Because after that fateful night, she'd moved out of his house and in with Dorian and Luke.

She went back to the children and lost herself in their antics and her instruction. But her own depression settled on her, like the sandstorms she'd witnessed from the Domes, blocking out all that was good and warm in her life.

• • •

HIS BOYS ALWAYS cheered him up, so David had made a plan to spend more time with them. He'd invited them to a World Series baseball game in the Bronx, took them to an amusement park and, tonight, was cooking a spaghetti dinner for them at church. They'd groaned about all his attention, but he knew they liked it. Interestingly, Brian Young had asked to help out. He still hadn't found a church, but wanted to work with youth, especially now that they didn't have Hal as a backup. He'd mentioned at the picnic he'd been talking to Jase, and the other boys had taken to him, too; right now, he was off getting the dessert a local bakery was donating.

As David stirred the sauce, he thought of how Alisha had disliked the dish when she first came to this time period but had eventually become acclimated to the taste. Just as she'd become acclimated to a lot of things—even making love with him.

Hell! The mere thought of her made his body respond. He missed her with a need so great sometimes it consumed him. But he hadn't contacted her. He'd been glad she'd moved out of his house so he didn't have to run into her. Though, truth be told, he was worried about her, especially after he'd met Dorian for coffee yesterday…

"How is she?" he'd asked her friend, once they'd gotten their drinks and without any preamble.

Dorian stared over at him with those piercing green eyes, making him want to shrink into his seat. "She's absolutely miserable. And she won't talk to me. I don't even know what happened between you two."

"She accused me of trying to seduce her into finding the arsonist on her computeller."

"Oh, by the godheads. Oh, no." Dorian's eyes moistened. "What's is it?"

"I put that idea into her head. It was a defense of you — I was saying that couldn't be the reason you'd made love with her. Oh, David, if that caused her to accuse you, it's because of me."

Reaching out, he'd grasped Dorian's hand. "No, Dorian, none of this is your fault. It's fate. I'm coming to believe she and I weren't meant to be together. But please, try to help her…"

Someone came up to him, pulling him out of the memory. "Hey, Rev."

David turned to see Jase Carpenter had entered the kitchen. Hell, he thought he'd locked the outer door. He wasn't being careful enough, as the arsonist was still on the loose. "There you are. I wondered what happened to my sous chef."

Because he was also worried about Jase, David had spent even more time with the boy than with the other five. The police had backed off on their accusations of arson, and Jase was now living with an aunt in the area because he hadn't been asked by his parents to go back home.

David had addressed the issue of Jase being gay, which the boy confirmed, so he'd gotten Jase into some groups and counseling sessions. Brian, whose brother was gay and whom Jase liked a lot, had taken the boy to PFLAG — a national organization designed for parents and friends of lesbians and gays. Brian also found a place that held support groups for gay teens.

"I was late getting out of a group meeting." He shrugged. "I met some more kids today and we're gonna hang out."

"That's great, Jase."

"Yeah. So, what's my chore?"

"Make the salad."

The boy went to the fridge and began removing lettuce and other vegetables. "How many guys comin'?"

"Six. It'll be fun. They're bringing movies."

"R-rated?" Jase teased.

"Nope. Action flicks."

Jase went to work but talked, which David appreciated. "Thanks for doing all this for us. Even when you're sad about Reverend Hal."

David still suffered from the loss of his friend, but recently, Alisha's departure from his life had tripled that grief. All the time, it seemed, making him tired as hell and cranky. But he put those thoughts aside as he tried to enjoy the meal, and then later, watch the movies. They were funny in places and had the kids in stitches. The idiom made him choke back emotion. He had to look away from a dark-haired woman who resembled Alisha. And he was struck by the notion that he might never stop making associations with her, missing her, craving her next to him at night.

So he prayed to God to help him cope and to take care of Alisha.

This time he got a direct response. *I sent you to her to take care of her, David. How's that going for you?*

• • •

ALISHA WATCHED THE red numbers on the clock turn from one to eleven p.m. She hadn't slept well since she'd broken everything off with David so tonight she'd fallen asleep right after dinner and now was awake.

Throwing off the covers, she sat on the side of the bed and buried her face in her hands. Every time she did sleep, the nightmares about David's death haunted her for hours — and sometimes plagued her for days — afterward. She simply couldn't tolerate the notion that he might die. Not when she could prevent it.

The realization came to her with acute clarity! And certainty. Nothing worse could happen than David's death. She knew that in her soul.

Taking a deep breath, she crossed to the dresser in Dorian's spare room and opened the bottom drawer. Took out one of the three computellers she'd confiscated and stored away. She set it down on the desk in the corner. It booted in seconds.

She hadn't used it in weeks. "Call up chip for the eighth month to the end of 2014. Specifically, Brooklyn, New York, fires."

"Working," the now unfamiliar voice said.

Seized by a bolt of panic at what she might discover, she shivered in her thin pajamas. But she kept David's beloved face in her mind. Finally, the computer stopped. "Information on the series of fires at the end of 2014 is ready. Five are reported."

Five? There had been another one.

"Name them."

The computer spat out the list of churches. St. Peter's Catholic Church on Lincoln Avenue; Ashbury Presbyterian, First Universalist Church on Hook Street(twice), and Community Christian Church on Lake Avenue.

The room spun. Alisha grabbed the desk's edge, but the whirring didn't stop. After a few minutes, she regained some equilibrium and asked, "W-who was injured in these fires?"

"Father Allen Kramer. Reverend Kerry Mackenzie. Reverend Hal Hanson. Reverend David Ryan."

She gasped. She couldn't talk. But she had to. "What happened to David Ryan?"

The computer clicked. And clicked. And clicked. "Negative information. The chips are experiencing corrosion for the next six months." They'd had that problem in saving Jess and taking care of Alex's research, too.

"Search David Ryan, pastor, in any time period after the chips begin again."

The computeller made grating noises. "No reports on David Ryan after the fire."

Alisha's stomach roiled, making her bolt up, rush to the bathroom and retch violently. Shakily, she made her way back to the machine. Sat down. And asked like an automaton, "Computeller, who set the fires?"

• • •

SHIVERING SOME IN the mid-October night—he'd forgotten to throw on a jacket over his jeans and T-shirt—David knocked on Luke and Dorian's door at about midnight. He knew it was too late to be calling, but he couldn't get his mind off the fact that he wasn't taking good care of Alisha, as God had asked of him. And he wanted to. Now, he was certain of that. So he'd come to her.

Luke finally drew open the door. His hair was disheveled and his eyes heavy lidded. "David?"

"I'm sorry I woke you. But this is urgent."

"Come on in. Dorian went to bed early, and I laid down with her. Guess I fell asleep, too. What's up?"

"I need to see Alisha."

"All right." Without asking questions, Luke headed down a corridor.

David waited, his heart beating a wild tattoo.

Luke returned quickly. "She's not here, David. She must have gone out."

"On a date?"

Luke shook his head. "You got it bad, buddy. But I don't think she had a date. She was here for dinner and went to her room right after. Said she had some work to do." He ran a hand through his hair. "You two need to talk to each other."

"Which is why I came. Any idea where she went?"

"Nope, there was no note in her room."

He deflated. Adrenaline had been shooting through him like a drug since he decided he wasn't letting Alisha go. Hell, why had it taken him so long? Now, the high was plummeting. "Okay. I'm sorry I bothered you."

"Want to stay and talk?" his friend asked.

"No, not to you. Thanks, anyway."

Even more despondent than before, David drove home. It had started to rain and he skidded — he was going too fast. He had to slow down, which made him think more about the empty house next door, without her in it.

But when he reached the duplex and spotted her Prius in the driveway, his entire system went on alert. Exiting the car quickly, he crossed to her half and knocked hard. She opened it right away. "Oh, David. David."

She looked about ready to explode. So overcome with emotion at seeing her, at knowing she'd come to him, too, he grabbed her, took her into his arms, and held her tight. "Lisha, love." They just hugged. Alisha trembled the entire time. To calm her down, he whispered, "I went to Dorian's. Looking for you. I couldn't stand another minute of separation."

She drew back and he could see she'd been crying.

"Oh, honey." He eased her inside and closed the door. Then he reached for her again.

She buried her head in his chest and mumbled, "I came here because of you, too."

"I'm so glad."

She pulled back away. "No, David, you won't be glad. Not at all."

"Well, I'll tell you one thing, if you think I'm letting you go again after we both were driven to see each other, you're crazy."

"It's not that." She sucked in a heavy breath. "I went on the computeller, like you asked. I found out what church was going to be hit next. And who the arsonist is."

• • •

ALISHA HELD TIGHT to David's hand as they walked up the brick path to the little suburban house. The only sign that a minister lived here was a small fish—a symbol of Christ—next to the doorbell. He rang it with a weariness that broke Alisha's heart; both knew what was about to transpire would be brutal. But she vowed to be strong for David.

Brian Young answered the door. His life was about to be shattered, too. He was fully dressed though, and Lisha noted another car in his driveway. "Hi, Brian."

"David. It's late. Is something wrong?"

"Yes, Brian," David said softly. "Something's terribly wrong."

Jeb Morse appeared behind Brian. David had told her the two men had been living together in Brian's house to save money. "David, is that you?"

"Hi, Jeb. We need to talk to you both."

Once inside, they settled in the living room, and if the two men thought it odd Alisha had tagged along, neither showed it. Both men sat on one couch, and Alisha dropped down on the other with David. The room was simple, sparsely furnished but homey.

David said simply, "I know you're the arsonist."

Brian's eyes widened. "Me? I'm not the arsonist."

"No, you aren't." Jeb sat forward. "But I am. And half of me is glad somebody finally knows."

"And the other half?" David asked.

"Is crazy as a loon."

• • •

JOE DESTINO WAS a professional, but in deference to David, he didn't handcuff Jeb. With a captain on Special Crimes in the NYPD, Joe met David, Alisha, Brian and, of course, Jeb, at the front door of the Brooklyn precinct. They asked for an interrogation room and calmly, kindly, escorted Jeb to it. The three lay people were allowed to watch from the outside. Though it was a break in protocol, the police agreed to let them hear the conversation at Destino's request.

As the captain read Jeb his rights, Brian said, "I can't believe this. Jeb and I had gotten close, spent so much time together and I didn't know."

"You know one side of Jeb." David's voice was gravelly. "He said himself that he's two people, has two sides to his personality, I guess."

Alisha interrupted them. "They're talking. Maybe we'll find out more now."

They knew little, because all Jeb had said after he confessed in Brian's living room was, "Please, take me to the police station. Let's get this over with."

"For the record, you've been read your Miranda rights and refused a lawyer, is that correct?" the policeman asked.

"Yes."

Joe took over then. "And you freely admit to setting four fires at St. Peter's Catholic Church, Ashbury Presbyterian and two at First Universalist."

His face blank, Jeb answered rotely. "Yes, I set them all."

"I'd like you to go through each occurrence and explain what you did to cause these fires." Both the cop and Joe had gotten out a notepad and began to write as soon as Jeb spoke again.

David listened to Jeb's confession. Each recounting was specific and detailed. The whole scene was surreal to David. And so sad he could barely listen to Jeb's words.

After nearly an hour, Joe asked, "Reverend Morse, can you tell us why you did these things?"

Suddenly, Jeb's whole body language changed. He raised his chin and his shoulders straightened. "Because I'm God's loyal servant and He told me to."

All three onlookers gasped.

The dialogue from then on was, well, spooky.

When the interrogation was finally over, the police captain stood. "Jeb Morse, you're under arrest for the murder of Hal Hanson and the crime of arson on four counts. Please stand."

Poor Jeb stood. They handcuffed him now. Joe walked to the door and out to the hallway. He was shaking his head. "Something's really odd here. He seemed like a different person when he explained his motive."

"He told us he was, Captain Destino," Brian answered. It's creepy."

Just then the door opened again, and the captain brought out Jeb. They stood in front of David.

"May I speak to him?" David asked.

"Go ahead."

David put his hand on Jeb's arm. "I'm here for you, Jeb. So is Brian. We'll help you through this."

Jeb's face was completely relaxed, though his eyes were glazed. "I don't need your help, David. Or yours, Brian. I was doing God's work. He'll take care of me."

Silenced, they watched Jeb and the officer walk down the hall.

"Sorry, buddy. I know this is hard for you." Joe clasped David's shoulder, then followed the other two.

Brian sighed. "I need to call the Ministerial Group. I don't want them hearing this on television."

"Go ahead. I'll be around if you need me." David couldn't make any calls himself. Too much had happened lately and immobility was setting in.

When he realized he and Alisha were alone, he took her hand and led her to the exit. Once they were in the car, he leaned back and closed his eyes. They remained silent, holding hands again when Alisha's cell phone rang.

"I have to get this." Alisha slid out her cell. "It's probably Luke. They might be worried."

"Of course."

"Hello. Oh, Dorian, hi." A startled gasp. *"What?"*

David glanced over at her. Her face had gone sheet white.

"I…I don't know what to say… All right, we'll go to Jess's right now."

"Did something happen to Helen?" David asked, expecting the worst.

"No. Not to Helen."

"Something's wrong."

She looked at him, dazed. "Jess was working late...very late tonight. And, David, oh, David, Rhea Hart appeared in his office, just like we did five months ago."

"Rhea Hart?"

"Celeste's donor. One of the ten Guardians in the future who sent us here."

"How is that possible? What does that *mean*?"

Her voice was hoarse when she said, "That I changed the future again by finding out the identity of the arsonist."

# CHAPTER 15

ALISHA WAS STUNNED at Dorian's news that Rhea was here. In this time period. She'd summoned Celeste, too. The Lansings left Virginia in the middle of the night and drove the two hours to arrive approximately when Alisha and David would.

"What are you thinking about all this?" David asked as they pulled onto Jess's street. David looked...battered. His face was lined with fatigue and grief, and his entire body slumped.

"I'm shocked. We were told there was only a tiny chance we'd be able to return to the future. That things would have changed too much. We might not even be remembered. For a long time, I hoped they were wrong; I hoped someone would come back and get us. No one did. Until now." But Rhea was here and despite her worry about what she'd done yet again to change the future, Alisha could barely contain her excitement.

They reached the Cromwell house and pulled up behind Alex's van in the driveway—the Lansings had just shut the engine off. Alisha bounded out of David's car.

Celeste climbed from the van and hugged her. "Can you believe it, Lisha? Rhea's *here*. I'll actually get to see her again. I'm so happy."

Extending the hug, Alisha whispered, "Me, too."

The two of them walked hand in hand up the steps and onto the front porch, the men speaking softly behind them.

Dorian whipped the door open before they could ring the bell. "Lisha? Celi? By the godheads."

Celeste said, "Where is she? I have to see her."

From behind her, Alex shrugged. "I tried to keep her calm, but she's too excited."

They all went inside and found Rhea in the living room, talking quietly with Luke and Jess.

"Rhea?" Celeste's voice shook.

Rhea looked up, then stood. Like a camera focusing in on a character, Alisha noticed Rhea's auburn hair was longer. Slim and fit, she wore the gray tunic and pants of their time, but the outfit was softened with pastel colors shot throughout the material. Her eyes widened when she saw her offspring. "Oh, Celi."

The women ran to each other and embraced. Rhea held Celeste for a long time, kissed her hair. "My love is yours, Celi."

Burying her head in Rhea's shoulder, Celeste choked out, "My love is yours, too."

After a moment, Rhea's eyes widened and she stepped back. "Celi, you're pregnant."

Dorian had joined them. "I'm pregnant, too, Rhea. I wanted to wait until Celi got here before I told you."

She put her hand on Celeste's stomach first, then Dorian's. "When will you give birth?"

Celeste was practically breathless. "Not until the spring. Dorian not long after." Over their shoulders, Rhea caught a glimpse of Alisha. "Lisha, dear, come join us."

Another group hug which felt good—and needed—with Alisha.

Then Rhea took Celeste's hand. "You're so lovely, Celi. All the Guardians will be glad to see you—all of you—when we get back."

"Get back?" Celeste asked.

"Of course. I came to bring you three back to your own time period." She raised her chin. "And to collect the computellers."

Luke stood and Alex also got to his feet. "My wife is not going anywhere," Luke said.

"Nor is mine."

Rhea watched Alex. "You are Celi's mate?"

"Yes."

"I see." She faced the women. "Don't you want to come back to your own time period? I never imagined you'd prefer to stay in this primitive society." The last phrase was uttered with distaste.

Celeste looked to Alex and smiled, then back to Rhea. "I can't go back, Rhea. I could never leave Alex or our three other children."

"You have more youngers?" Rhea asked. "Is that possible in such a short time period?"

"We have younglings from Alex's first marriage. I consider myself their mother now."

Though not a sensitive, Alisha was struck with a thought. "Are there younglings in the future?"

"Of course, but we call them a shortening of what you say."

Dorian sidled next to Luke. "I'm staying, too. But, Rhea, we have so much to ask you."

"Which I'll answer. But first..." She turned to Alisha. "What about you? Will you return with me?"

Alisha just stood there, trying to internalize this latest development in a night fraught with shock and sadness.

But she didn't say no.

• • •

KATHRYN SHAY

DAVID FELT A coldness invade him and thought he was probably going into shock. The events of the evening had thrown him into chaos, and now everything he thought might happen, once Alisha had come to him tonight, once she'd discovered the identity of the arsonist for him, was clouded by Rhea's return. But he pretended things were fine, crossed to Alisha and drew her aside. "Honey, are you all right?"

She moved in close to him, leaned on him. "I am. Are you? You've had a rough night."

"I'm okay. Why don't you introduce me to Rhea?"

Rhea stepped closer. "Hello, I'm Rhea Hart. I'm Celeste's mother."

"Mother?" Alisha's mouth gaped. "You use that term?"

"When children are birthed from a woman's womb, we do. If the child is conceived in the produceries, they often prefer the term donors."

"So society has changed?" Celeste asked, glancing at Alex. "There's no more infertility?"

"We went through a period of that, but centuries before. In modern times, we give birth if we choose." She glanced at Celeste. "As I did Celi."

In her peripheral vision, Alisha saw Alex close his eyes. She imagined he was thinking that the sacrifice of his work had been successful. And worth all he'd given up.

Rhea addressed David. "You're Alisha's spouse? All three of you have joined?"

"Excuse me?" David croaked out.

"Joined. Committed your life to each other."

The three women exchanged looks. Joining meant something different in the future?

"Not all of us are joined." David reached out a hand. "I'm Reverend David Ryan."

212

Rhea clasped it. The custom of handshaking had made it to the twenty-sixth century. "Reverend?" Rhea's brow furrowed. "The ancient term for clergy."

"What term do you use now?"

"We have no term. We have no clergy."

David froze. Could this be? There was still no religion in the future, though so much had changed? Before he could ask, Helen entered the room, interrupting them.

"I've rested, as you insisted, Jess, but I prepared some tea and coffee. I think everybody could use it."

Celeste asked, "Rhea...Mother..." Her face bloomed. "Do you have coffee and tea in the future?"

"Of course we do. For special occasions."

When they were seated with their drinks, Rhea took over, and David realized she was used to being in control of the situation. "As I said, I teleportaled to this time period to retrieve you three and also to secure your computellers."

The Sisters of Doom remained silent, as if accustomed to listening to Rhea.

"And as I indicated, our society has changed."

"We were hoping it would, Rhea," Dorian told her. "That's why you sent us back. To alter the future."

"I remember certain things about society before that happened, and of course, the history 1.0 chips filled us in. Giving birth to Celeste is recorded differently on the 1.0 chips from the 2.0 ones. We also kept a detailed recounting of sending you back in time."

Alisha frowned. "Two-point-oh chips?"

"Yes. But you wouldn't know of those because they were a result of the changes you made per the Guardians' instructions. We're in possession of the history chips before and after you left." She arched a brow. "Then, just recently, we discovered we had another set. We call them 3.0."

"I'm confused." This from Jess.

"What that means is that my girls changed society three times."

Alisha grasped David's hand and he held it tight. She'd do it over again, but this was the worst possible outcome.

Regally, Rhea continued. "When we discovered the 2.0 chips, we were satisfied with the results, though in real time, we knew nothing else. We were on the verge of banning all time travel. Then, before we could destroy the elements of teleportation, more things changed. Those changes were subtle, so we remembered most of what was on the 2.0 chips, and this time we knew what happened right away."

"Then how do you remember me if at first you didn't remember the 1.0 chips?" Celeste asked. "That I'm your daughter?"

"I just do. We think it's a genetic imprint. Residual memories. And I recall that I gave birth to you, but the 1.0 chips indicated you were conceived in the producerie. It's all quite a paradox, something we accept about time travel."

"Am I...am I *in* the future?" Celeste asked.

"No, none of you are. But we have the recorded chips to verify your existence. And I've been saddened by the loss of you, Celi, so when we knew we had to retrieve the computellers, I came to get you, too."

"She's not going back." Alex's voice was firm.

Luke slid his arm around Dorian possessively. "You can't have Dorian either."

Rhea smiled. "I can see that now. And it's acceptable to me."

"How did you find them?" Helen asked.

"I waited for another portal to open and teleportaled to the same time period and place the Guardians—we—had sent you. It was Jess's work space."

"Hell of a thing," Jess said, shaking his head. "Déjà vu. She appeared exactly as you three did. Only this time, I didn't think I'd lost my mind. I brought her right here."

"And you say you came to stop more interference with the future?" Alex asked.

"Yes. We were satisfied that you'd accomplished your tasks. We achieved our goals. But then, other things changed."

"Because of what I did tonight, right?"

Rhea focused on her. "More than likely, Lisha."

"What did you do tonight?" Dorian asked.

Alisha hesitated. She hadn't told anybody that she'd found the identity of the arsonist. Or that David had been hurt.

• • •

AFTER ANOTHER HOUR of discussion, everybody was tired and knew they should get some sleep. Alisha, Celeste and Dorian took the guys to their former rooms downstairs. Rhea was installed in the den, where Alisha headed after David fell into a deep sleep. Rhea had left the den door ajar.

"I knew you'd come, Alisha." Looking only minimally fatigued by the jump, Rhea patted the spot next to her on the bed. They sat facing each other.

"I couldn't sleep."

"I'm not surprised." She studied Alisha. "Tell me about your man, David."

"He's a minister."

Rhea searched her face. "Do you believe in this god, Alisha?"

She opened her mouth to deny it, to declare that God was nothing but the figurehead they'd thought God to be in the future, but her mind objected. *Say what's in your heart, Alisha.*

And suddenly, she knew. The realization had been coming for a long time. "Yes, I do, Rhea."

"Interesting. How did you come to believe this?"

"Talking with David. Reading. Seeing how people of today are affected by their beliefs." She didn't reveal to Rhea the conversations she had with God. "In my heart, I simply know of a supreme being's existence."

"Is it helpful, to believe like this?"

"It's crucial to David."

Reaching out, she touched Alisha's arm. "And to you?"

"It's new to me. I'm not sure." She smiled. "Can I ask you some things about the future?"

"Always."

"You're so calm about what's happened. Even my changing the future again today."

"We're all calm in 2514. Society went through great turmoil, but we've come out on the other side. We're...settled. And happy."

"We weren't happy when I left, Rhea. We were just trying to survive."

"So I gathered from the 1.0 chips. I'm sorry to know you existed in that way in our time. But you altered the past and the future is brighter. What questions do you have?"

"You said women can have babies now."

"Of course. But, again, from viewing the 1.0 chips, I know we couldn't when you left. The 2.0 chips show you and Celeste and Dorian succeeded in stopping the research that led to our fertility problems."

"You met the man whose research we sabotaged. And Jess, the one we saved."

"Jess and I talked about that before you arrived. And I knew Alex's name because I assigned you to destroy his research. He wasn't angry at what you'd done?"

"Of course he was. But Alex is a good man and he helped me alter the needed sections. Then he fell in love with Celeste and got over his anger at us. What about air pollution? Do we still have the Domes?"

Rhea shook her head. "Society began to build them when it seemed we were headed for extinction. But they were never completed and eventually torn down."

"Once we saved Jess's life."

"Yes. It's all very fascinating. He's on the 2.0 chips as having been the father of zero-pollution index."

"You have to tell him that."

"I did." She grinned. "He and Helen were delighted."

"Did we have war?"

"Chips 1.0 show the first time around, we had horrible cyber wars destroying most of the population. But chips 2.0 show those were contained to the twenty-second century, and not as virulent. We do still have a smaller population, because many people were killed then and there were some fertility issues."

"And the 3.0 chips? I didn't change any of that, did I?"

"No, but subtle things changed. Some minor differences in transportation methods. Some language variables. Oddly enough, clothing became colored."

Celeste would love that.

"How are younglings raised?"

"Not by one person or even a couple, though there's some movement toward nuclear families. Youngers come to live with their parents at the age of five, and even when they're still in the produceries, mothers and fathers are more active in their lives. But we consider all of society responsible for the health and well-being of the next generation." Again, she squeezed Alisha's arm. "That's all very good, dear. I cannot see the benefit of raising youngers—children—as people do today."

Suddenly, Alisha wondered who her father was. Her mother had been a wonderful woman but died from an accident when Alisha was ten.

"What about joining?"

"I mentioned that joining is a commitment ceremony between two people to be sexual only with each other. I must confess, it's not very popular."

The thought made her warm. She felt the need for commitment to David. "Did you commit to Celi's father?"

"I did." Now Rhea rolled her eyes. "He vehemently voiced his concern about my transporting to the twenty-first century, but he also badly wanted Celeste to return."

"Are all these things consistent throughout the world?"

"The world isn't as large, as I said, but yes, they're consistent."

"That's amazing. What about technology? Are we still as advanced?"

"Oh, just wait until you hear this story."

• • •

DAVID AWOKE AT dawn and reached for Alisha. She was his lifeline now. But her side of the bed was empty, her indentation on the mattress light. Then he remembered. Hal was dead, Jeb had committed the arson. And Rhea Hart had come to take the Sisters of Doom home. He lay back on the pillow and sighed. Where would he get the strength to deal with all this? From God, of course, who would be with him. He closed his eyes and prayed.

After a while, he was able to rise, dress and climb the stairs. The house was quiet as he went looking for Alisha on the first floor, then outside, but he couldn't find her. Until he passed the den. The door was ajar, so he peeked in. Alisha lay facing Rhea, their hands clasped, both sound asleep. He hoped the fact that she'd left him to go to Rhea wasn't an omen.

If it was, he couldn't deal with that now. Closing the door gently, he found his car keys and left Jess's house. First, he went to church to pray some more, then he returned home. He'd write his sermon for tomorrow.

His people needed him. All the churches in the area would be in flux after last night's discovery; some of his own congregants might know what had happened, some not. There had been many messages left on his phone, which he'd return later today. David needed to phrase everything correctly in the sermon so he could lead them through this horrid time. Had Hal been alive, he would have gone to him for guidance.

But Hal was dead.

Sitting down at his desk, he let the words come to him from God, as they always did. He wrote about people and their frailties, about mental illness. He quoted the Bible with examples. As a psychologist, he'd tell them he believed Jeb had had a psychotic break, perhaps was borderline schizophrenic. Perhaps something else. But Jeb had been a good man, who'd succumbed to a dark side of himself. They all needed to forgive him. David had just written the last word when his doorbell rang.

When he opened the door, Alisha stood before him looking animated, excited, optimistic. He'd never once seen the expression so purely on her face.

"Hi," he said, managing a smile. "Big night, huh?"

"It was. I'm so sorry about Jeb. We didn't even have time to talk about him. And before that, there was much to discuss."

"Come on in."

She'd showered and changed, and her scent wafted over him as she stepped inside. "We need to talk."

"I know. Let's go to the porch. It's cool but pleasant."

When they were settled, he asked, "Where do we start?"

"With what happened to us at Celi's before the world caved in."

"Ah." Even now, his body heated at the reminder of what had happened on that couch in Alex's den.

He stated firmly, "We made love."

"We did." It surprised him that she agreed. "And I discovered something."

*Here it comes.* He'd be strong, if it killed him.

"My love is yours, David. In your words, I love you. And what's more, I'm not upset about our relationship. I want this kind of connection with you."

The vise in his heart loosened and his eyes moistened. "I-I never expected this."

"It's true."

*Don't be too optimistic,* he told himself. "But there's more, isn't there?"

"Oh, David, I talked to Rhea all night. She told me wonderful things about the future."

"Like?"

"Mankind made progress in similar ways as the first time around, before we changed the future. But because we saved Jess and ended Alex's research, in 2300, they saw they were on a collision course to disaster and scaled back on everything.

They still gave up the body implant, got a grip on the carbon index and carefully monitored drugs dealing with sexuality."

"I'm glad you accomplished your goals."

"Society learned its lesson. From that and the cyber wars, which did happen early on."

He listened with awe and with deepening disappointment. "But there is still no religion. Rhea confirmed that. They have no clergy, still use *godheads*."

"I'm sorry, David. That's all true. But there's some good news regarding that. The belief in God is starting to return to society. Rhea told me they found several sacred tomes — the Bible, the Torah, the Talmud, the Koran — in an excavation of what used to be New York."

"What happened when they found the good books?"

"Pockets of believers started to spring up. Rhea says God is taking hold and religion is...reappearing. It's happening, David."

He breathed a sigh of relief. "I'm grateful for that."

"You can make it better."

"What do you mean?"

Her lovely face shone with hope and a bit of awe. "I want you to go back to the future with me and Rhea. The next portal opens in three weeks. We can both go. You can help bring religion to the people of my time."

"Why would you even want that, honey? You're not a believer."

She sighed, closed her eyes briefly. "Because I not only discovered my love is yours, David, but something else. I sense the existence of some kind of Supreme Being, who I'd like to embrace."

She believed! She actually believed. Somewhere in his mind, he'd been holding back the notion of whether he could be with a woman who didn't accept, in some form, the most important thing in his life. "That makes me as happy as knowing you love me."

She watched him. "Do you love me, David?"

"Of course I do. I have for a long time." Reality wormed its way into his euphoria. "But, honey, I can't go to the future."

"Yes. Yes, you can. I haven't told you everything. Your church was hit by the arsonist the first time around. You were hurt. I don't know how badly, because the chips got corroded."

David was speechless.

"There's no record of you by the time I got a clear chip."

His insides turned cold. "I died? Like Jess originally did?"

"Maybe. But maybe not. Maybe you went to the future with me. To live there. That's why there's no record of you in the intervening years."

"That doesn't make sense. Was I not on the 3.0 chips?"

"Rhea had no reason to check for you, because she knew nothing about our involvement."

"I can't wrap my brain around this."

"No one can. Time travel is ephemeral. Even scientists and fiction writers of your time couldn't fully grasp it."

"What did Rhea say about it all?"

"She cited the paradox of time travel, David, the same as you did when you wanted me to look for the arsonist. We came back and were supposed to effect the changes we did. It was meant to be. Including saving your life, if that's what happened. Don't you see, David, you're *supposed* to come to the future with me."

"I don't know what to say."

She clasped his hands. Held them tight. "Then I'll quote you. *Have faith*. Return to the future with me, be our...prophet, I think you call it in your time."

David looked at her, wanting to be with her more than he could say. But he knew the answer to her question, deep in his heart, and it pained him greatly. "I can't, Lisha. My people need me here. There will be repercussions of untold consequences because of what happened in the Brooklyn churches. I can't abandon all of them in their time of need."

Silent, she seemed puzzled. "You'll abandon me, instead?"

"No. Stay here with me. Marry me. We can live out our lives in this time period, together."

He saw the answer on her face before she even spoke the words.

# CHAPTER 16

"WE HAVE *NOTHING* like this in our time." Rhea licked the chocolate ice cream from its cone. Alisha loved watching her experience new things since she'd come to their time. They sat outside of a gelato place in downtown Brooklyn, enjoying the cool day and each other.

Celeste winked. "We'll send the recipe for how to make it back with you." The words at the end of her sentence came out hoarse, accompanied by a few tears. "I'm sorry I'm so emotional, but I'm going to miss you, Rhea. Again." She turned to Alisha. "And you."

Five days ago, Alisha had refused to stay in 2014 with David, and he'd refused to go with her to 2514. They were at what was called a stalemate, and she knew in her heart, neither one of them would give in.

"What are you thinking, Lisha?"

She shook her head. "Take a wild guess."

Everything was out on the table now. She'd told the women all of what had happened between her and David. But since then, when she tried to talk about it, she couldn't.

"Have you seen him?"

Swallowing hard, she pictured David in bed last night, his body rising above her, his powerful arms pulsing with his weight, declaring his love. "Yes. We spend as much time together as we can."

"Isn't it hard?" Dorian asked. "Don't you fight about what each of you has decided? Every time Luke and I disagree, he tries to convince me he's right."

"No, we promised each other we wouldn't fight. That we'd enjoy what time we had left. David taught me how to do that."

As did God. She was talking to the deity a lot these days. God seemed to want her to go back to her time. Or was she just making herself believe that? Sometimes, this God-stuff got complicated.

She turned to Rhea. "Tell us more about the little things in the future, so I know."

They had real food, but it was low in fat and carbohydrates and people ate only one meal of it a day. Supplements were taken in place of other meals. "You have no treats like ice cream?"

"No. It is bad for your body-fat index and arteries." Rhea smiled when she made the weak complaint.

Celeste grinned. "You'll like that people are still fitness conscious, Lisha. Of all of us, you stayed on the supplements the longest and hated to give them up. I *love* this time period's food."

Alisha smiled, too, but with a sadness so great it swamped her. "I got used to most of the meals."

"I want to know more about the clothing." Dorian had finished off her cone. "I've become enamored of lingerie."

Rhea cocked her head. "I have no idea what that is."

"Oh, damn."

When they explained, she said, "We still sleep naked. Even when we're alone. And I'm afraid we don't use clothing as enticements."

Celeste was ruminating. "I'm so glad sex between people is meaningful. We lost something precious in the future the first time around."

"So the 1.0 chips reveal," Rhea remarked. "And yes, I wouldn't have wanted to live with anonymous sexual relationships." She winked at Celeste. "Your father and I are very close."

Of all the things that had changed, the sexual customs were the most different. There was no SexLine, but computellers still computed the best matches for people. However, on their meetings, there was no expectation of sex. If that came naturally, fine. Otherwise, just like now, they enjoyed the companionship and where it might lead them.

The topic led Alisha to thoughts of David, and her future. He would make love to other women, and she'd most likely have sex with other men—though she could barely tolerate the thought of someone else touching her like David did.

Celeste must have noticed. "Alisha, talking about sex makes you sad, I can tell."

"I—"

Holding up her hand, Celi ordered, "Tell me the truth."

"Yes. Now that I've been with David, I can't imagine wanting to be with someone else." She'd changed so much.

It was Rhea who broached the topic everyone else carefully avoided. "Are you sure you want to come with me, dear?"

"I am. It will be difficult leaving David, but I don't fit in here as Celi and Dorian do. I don't even *like* it. I want to be back in my own time."

Celeste said, "I understand."

And Dorian grabbed her hand.

Later, when Alisha left them, her sadness multiplied. Not only was she leaving David, but Celi and Dorian. Still, in her heart, she knew she wanted to go back—or forward. As she pulled up to the Refugee Center, she turned off the car and stared at the building.

She loved working in this place, with these younglings. Had she stayed, she would have turned down the museum job, as she'd done yesterday, for the children. But no matter how much it hurt, she needed to say good-bye to them today.

Kerry met her at the door. "Hello. Thanks for coming in to do this." The reverend had told her she'd try to explain the story Alisha had concocted to the children. Their original background information had been so convincing, the plan now was to tell everybody that she was going back to South America to pick up the work her missionary parents had done. That was acceptable. If anyone became suspicious about her disappearance, the others she was leaving behind would tell them they'd been in contact and she was doing fine.

Walking through the halls, Alisha wondered if schooling of the future was different. Anthropology probably wouldn't be as necessary. The Institutes didn't exist as before. Maybe she could become a professional teacher if they had them.

Kerry let her go into the room first, and Alisha stopped short. The children bolted up from the floor and yelled, "Surprise." The room was awash with color—paper streamers hanging from the ceilings, handmade signs from the children, some refreshments in the corner. The scent of baked goods rose up to meet her, too.

Behind the food table stood David, his arms folded over his chest, smiling at her. Thank God—and she did mean that—they were being kind to each other about their choices.

"What's all this?" she asked the children.

Abdefatah ran toward her and hugged her tightly. "You leaving, Missy Lisha. We don't want you to go."

And for a brief moment, Alisha didn't want to go either.

• • •

DAVID WATCHED ALISHA interact with the children—a woman who'd never had experience with them previous to her arrival in 2014. His heart was in a perpetual state of sadness, grief and longing for what had been—with Hal, Jeb and, of course, her. Still, he'd do this honorably if it killed him.

Sometimes, in the dark of night, when she lay beside him, he thought it might.

She made her way to him, wearing jeans and a plain white shirt. Idly, he wondered if they had denim in the future. "Hi," she said with the phoniest smile he'd ever seen. He knew she was suffering, too.

"They wanted to say *bon voyage.*"

"That's sweet. How are you? And the congregants of church?"

That she no longer called it *your* church, or referred to *your* God made him happy and despondent at the same time. They could have had so much together.

"Lee Ann and I made it a point to see each member of the congregation after Hal's death. Brian helped us, too. I think that helped. And I found out she's better at grief counseling than I am. For second visits or phone calls, most people have contacted her."

"Perhaps you were too involved in this whole thing to help others objectively."

"Maybe." Who the hell knew? He wasn't sure of much these days.

"What are you doing after this party?" she asked.

"I thought we could go for a bike ride, if you're free."

She smiled sweetly. Lovingly. "I want to spend as much time with you as I can, you know that."

"I feel the same way."

Kerry approached them. She stood by David and slid her arm around his waist. "How you doing, buddy? We all know you're taking this the hardest."

They knew he'd miss Alisha this much?

She added, "Our ministerial group is worried about you the most."

Oh. "Thank you. But I'll be fine." His gaze locked with Alisha's. Maybe.

After the party ended, they drove back to their home where she'd moved back, but this time, into his half, got the bikes and set out on a path they'd taken before. The wind blew cold on their faces. "I'm surprised I like the weather in this season, too," Alisha said from next to him. As they were going at a slow pace, they could still talk. "I'll miss it."

"We haven't discussed the future after our...decisions. There's still no seasons?"

"Nope. Because some global warming occurred, and other pollution, there's a similar climate all the time."

"Ah. Well, at least you can be out of indoors."

She smiled. "I never call it that anymore."

"They probably don't in the future, either."

"I suppose." They came to a place on the path with a long stretch. She pretended excitement. "Come on, let's race to the end." She took off fast.

He didn't. He watched her pedal away, just as she'd be leaving him in a couple of weeks. *Dear Lord in heaven, give me strength.*

In a few minutes, he found the will to follow her.

● ● ●

AFTER HE'D PICKED her up, he tossed her on the bed. She laughed aloud. They were trying to keep their lovemaking light and not have it tinged with the sadness neither one could escape.

He kissed his way down her body. Alisha closed her eyes and treasured the moment. "That tickles," she said when he lifted her leg and ran his tongue on the inside of her thigh. He continued the action until she was immersed in a fit of giggles.

"Ah, I'll miss that laugh." She stilled at the comment. They rarely spoke of their sadness. "Sorry, I didn't mean…"

"It's all right. I understand."

He got down to serious business then, arousing her in all the places he'd found to be her *hot spots,* he'd called them. Then he slid inside her and threaded his fingers through her hair. "I love you, Alisha. So much. I'll never, ever forget you." He pushed harder then, and sent her spiraling over the edge. When he joined her, she held on tight to him.

And burst into tears.

•  •  •

"EARNESTLY?" ALISHA SAID as she opened the door to her home and found David, in the entryway, dressed as a devil. "Isn't that counterproductive to your calling?"

Leaning over, he kissed her. The mask tickled her nose. "You look cute."

"I feel ridiculous." She'd let him pick out her costume, and, he'd chosen an angel. Her robe was white and filmy, and a garland encircled her head.

"Ready to go?" she asked.

"Yes. Thanks for coming to the party. I'm trying to make sure my boys are off the street tonight."

"Good idea." She winked at him, vowing they make the situation light. After she'd cried last night, he'd just held her and they didn't talk about the episode. What was there to say?

As they made their way out of the neighborhood, Alisha mused on the concept of Halloween. "This has to be the oddest holiday yet. I understand the origins of Christmas, Easter, Fourth of July. Days honoring veterans. But this one is pagan and doesn't really fit in your culture."

"In some ways, it does. Remember that *Star Trek* episode we watched, where once a year, the people of a town the crew visits have a festival and go crazy and let out all their...inner evil, I guess. In some ways, Halloween gives permission to people to walk on the dark side."

He'd already told her the origin of the day. A shortened version of All Hallows' Eve, for the night preceding All Saints Day, the celebration had its roots in the festivals of the dead, a pagan ritual, and the Celtic Samhain, which celebrated the end of the harvest and beginning of winter. She guessed his explanation made sense.

As they pulled up to the church, she saw the interior of the fellowship hall was lit up, meaning his associate pastor, Lee Ann, would be there. "Any other adults coming?"

"A few of the deacons. And Brian Young."

"How's he doing with the kids?" She knew that a few weeks ago, Brian had asked to work with the group of boys David had taken under his wing (though he wasn't a bird and they weren't baby birds). Brian had attended their gatherings regularly.

"Amazingly well. He relates best to Jase, who needs help, but the other guys *dig* him. We found out that Brian had a checkered past. Who would have known? He's so mild mannered. When it was appropriate, he shared some of his experiences with the kids. And he has tattoos, not visible because of his clothes. He's been a Godsend."

The notion was reinforced when they went inside and found Lee Ann and Brian in costume. Lee Ann had dressed as a rock star, and Brian wore jeans, boots, a leather jacket and revealed a few tattoos.

David burst out laughing when he saw him. "Nice costume," he said to the man, giving him an odd handshake. "Love the biker look."

Brian nodded. "Thought the kids could relate."

The boys arrived soon, grumbling at their *summons* to come to a church on Halloween, but it was clear they adored David. As Alisha watched him interact with them, her heart clutched. Tonight, she witnessed exactly what she'd asked him to give up. If she'd been holding out any hope he'd change his mind, it was quashed seeing David in his element.

• • •

DAVID PUT ON a good face for his church people, but each day he grew more and more morose, and it was harder and harder to keep his mood from everyone, most of all Alisha. But he guessed that was okay. She was leaving tomorrow.

As he taped the last of her boxes to go to charity, he surveyed the space. It was empty now of couches and chairs, fresh flowers, the scents and sounds of life. Two months ago, when she'd moved in, he'd been delighted. He'd had such hope for her.

*David, David, David, look how far she's come.*

God was talking to him regularly, trying to keep him company and cheer him up.

*I know she believes in You. That's the most important thing.* He waited. *She's really going back, isn't she?*

He didn't expect God to answer. Shouldn't have asked, but he heard loud and clear, *Yes, son, she is.*

Alisha came out of the kitchen with two beers. Though she hadn't appreciated most of their food and drink, she'd taken a liking to dark ale, as well as wine. They sat on the floor, leaning against the wall, and clinked bottles. "Thanks for your help."

"My pleasure. That family over on the East Side loves your furniture."

"I'm glad." She retrieved a box that sat against one wall. "I have another present for you."

He didn't want presents. He wanted her.

"Oh, goodie. What is it?"

"Open it."

About six-by-five inches, the small box was heavy. He lifted the lid. "Oh, Alisha, no. I can't accept these."

"Of course you can. Rhea said there's no money in the future, only credits in our time, like before. Diamonds will be worthless to me."

"Give them to Celi and Dorian for their kids."

"They insisted I take a third. I want you to have them to" — she narrowed her eyes as she took a sip of the beer — "do God's work in the world."

"I don't know what to say."

She put down the beer and straddled his lap. "Thank you would be good." She cocked her head. "But you know that truism, *Actions speak louder than words*? You could, um, show me how grateful you are."

David pulled her face to his chest. He'd taken the last three days off to be with her, and they'd made love several times. He couldn't get enough of her. When the dark thoughts started to consume him, he lifted her chin and kissed her.

He didn't know what else to do.

• • •

ON THE DAY of the portal opening, Rhea and the couples met at a little restaurant in downtown Brooklyn. Sitting at a round table covered in black, with sleek candles and musicals in the background, they sipped cocktails. After a farewell dinner, they'd go to Jess's office, where the jump would take place at midnight.

Luke set his drink down with too much force. "All right, I'll ask it. Where the hell is David?"

Dorian told her Luke had been really cranky this week, and she attributed it to Alisha leaving. He'd come to love her, after all.

"He said he'd be here and he will."

Which wasn't exactly the truth. Last night he'd said, *I'm not sure I can bear it. Watching you disappear into the future.*

She'd brushed back his beloved curls, sweaty from the exertion of making love. *Just come to the dinner. You don't have to watch the jump.*

David had nodded, but she'd had a feeling he might not show…

"I wouldn't come and watch Celi leave me. I couldn't." All gazes locked on Alex. He was so serene these days, happy with Celi and the kids, he rarely criticized anything.

"Alex?" Celeste asked.

He shook his head. "I've kept quiet about this long enough. I'm sorry, Alisha, Rhea, but it's crazy for Alisha to go back with you. She belongs with us now."

"I agree," Luke put in.

Jess did, too.

The Sisters of Doom, as Luke had dubbed them, exchanged looks. Only they knew the need to be a part of a world you were born into. Only they had experienced the wrenching sadness at having lost their...grounding.

Finally, Alisha spoke. "I'm sorry Alex, Luke, Jess. But you just don't understand."

Luke's face reddened. "Then why aren't you going back?" he asked Dorian.

"Don't be an ass. I love you; my life is here with you. But coming to your time, getting acclimated, was the hardest thing I've done. If I didn't have you all..." She scanned the table. "I'd go back, too."

"As would I." Celeste's tone was certain.

Luke threw down his napkin. "Come get some air with me, you guys."

Jess stood abruptly. "Since I happen to agree with what they said, I will." He zeroed in on Alisha. "I don't want you to leave us, Lisha." Then he stalked off.

When the women were alone, they focused on her.

Alisha blurted out, "David didn't know if he could handle tonight. I asked him just to come to the dinner, and he said he'd try. He's suffering so much, and I hate being the cause."

Rhea sighed. "You've all made so many connections here." She turned her troubled blue eyes on Alisha and took her hand. "Are you sure you want to come back? You have a few more hours to change your mind."

Staring at David's empty seat, Alisha sighed heavily.

• • •

ON THE EDGE of the pew in God's house, his head buried in his hands, David prayed for strength. He didn't ask for the oomph to go to the dinner to say good-bye to Alisha. No way could he keep up the front with all of them. In essence, he'd said his good-byes this morning.

Someone came down the church aisle. He looked up to see Lee Ann had reached his pew. "David, may I sit?"

"I'd prefer you didn't. I'm not doing well."

"I'm afraid I have to insist." She took a seat in the pew next to him. "What are you doing here at eleven o'clock at night?"

"I needed to be as close to God as possible. That always comforts me."

"I know you're suffering. I know Alisha's leaving. I've come to tell you you're not indispensable."

His brows raised. "Excuse me?"

"You heard me. You're so good, so kind and so unselfish. Too unselfish."

"No one can be too unselfish."

She smiled sadly at him. "Oh, yes, you can. I have a theory. If you get to a place where you're sacrificing all your needs for others, you become diminished. Slowly, over time."

"That's interesting. I wonder how Jesus would view that."

"Jesus would agree." Reaching out, she touched his hand. "Go with her."

"*What?*"

"To wherever she's going. And I don't believe for a second she's heading to South America. Something's been off about her since she came here, but it doesn't matter. Go with her."

"I can't leave my parishioners, the wider church in Brooklyn, when we're in such flux."

"That's not true. Don't you see? You—or God—has been preparing us for your departure. Bringing Brian in to work with the boys you love so much. Giving me a large part in healing this community. Even if the congregation didn't call me as their pastor if you were gone — which I think they would — your people will survive." Again the wise smile. "I'm not sure I can say the same thing for you if you let her go."

Sitting back in the pew, he closed his eyes. Exhausted, he said what he hadn't uttered since she decided to leave. "She should stay."

"Maybe she should. But apparently, she can't." Lee Ann waited. "Tell me something, David. Is there a place for you to bring God where she's going?"

*I'll quote you. Have faith. Return to the future with me, be our...prophet.*

"Like you wouldn't believe."

"That ought to make things easier." She stood and squeezed his arm. "I've said my piece. I'll leave and let you be alone with God."

"Lee Ann?" he called out when she was halfway down the aisle. "Despite my disagreeing with you, thanks for trying to help."

"Do you, David? Disagree?" She nodded to the altar. "It's not nice to lie in God's house."

• • •

AT ELEVEN THIRTY, the eight of them waited in Jess's office. A backpack containing all the computellers sat next to Alisha's feet. On either side of her, Celi and Dorian held her hands. But there was no chatter.

Finally, Luke broke the awful silence. "How does this happen? I mean, what does it look like? A big gaping hole that you step through like in *The Outer Limits?*"

Rhea held up her small computeller. "No. We set the dials to connect with the portal. Then there's a charge in the atmosphere in a specific space that indicates the portal. We simply step into it, and we're taken."

Jess nodded. "Like beaming up in *Star Trek*. That was my first thought when I saw you three arrive."

"So, nobody goes by mistake, right?" Alex asked, gripping Celeste's hand.

Rhea smiled benevolently. "No."

Twenty uncomfortable minutes later, Rhea declared, "It's time to say your good-byes."

The three men approached Alisha first.

Alex hugged her. She said, "Take care of Celi and the baby."

"I'll miss you. Thank you for bringing her to me."

Luke scowled at her. "Right till the fucking end, you're causing problems, aren't you?" But his eyes were bright and his hands shaking.

"Just like you, buddy."

His bear hug was so tight she thought he might break one of her ribs.

Jess was last. She was closest to him, and she felt her eyes mist. She said only, "Oh, Jess," and threw herself into his arms.

He brought Helen into the embrace.

"Good luck with Baby Jessica," she whispered.

In her ear, Helen said, "I hope you have a child one day, Lisha."

The notion was too much to consider without David.

When Celeste approached her, Alisha wondered if she could go through with this. She'd carry with her the image of Celi's strong build and contradictory delicateness, dressed, of course, in pink.

Celeste took her shoulders. "You can go through with this, honey. If it's what you want." Of course her friend had read her thoughts.

"I'm conflicted."

"I know you are." They hugged. "My love is yours, Lisha. Always."

"Mine is yours."

Crying, Celeste crossed to Alex.

Dressed in an emerald green, one-piece thing, Dorian took Celeste's place. Alisha would remember her much longer, beautiful hair and her strength, inside and out. "I don't know what I'll do without you."

"I feel the same, Dorian. Our relationship is very precious to me. Thank you for being my friend."

"Forever," she said. "Literally."

Stoically, Alisha glanced at the clock. Three minutes to the portal opening. She heard Rhea say, "It's time to get situated, Alisha."

Alisha had just turned away from the faces of the people she loved, when she heard. "Hold on! Not just yet."

Her heart sank. This was hard enough without David here. And paradoxically, she was so glad he'd come.

Dressed in dark pants and dark shirt, he carried the box of diamonds she'd given him and some papers. He glanced at the clock, then strode to Jess. "Here, use these as you see fit. And give these letters out to the people they're addressed to."

"I don't understand," Jess said.

"You will. There's one for you." He faced everybody and waved. "No time for hugs. I love you all."

Then he went to Alisha and took her hand.

Weak with shock and sadness, Alisha couldn't move. "David, I don't understand."

"I'm coming with you, love. I'd live in any time, past, present or future as long as I'm with you." He kissed her nose. "I'll explain why when we get there."

Then the lights dimmed, and the air in the room crackled as though lightning had struck. The temperature spiked. Sparks shot out from nowhere.

Alisha and David stepped into the unknown.

# EPILOGUE

DAVID STARED OVER at the structure as the last brick was set in place. He smiled, hugely, at this incredulous accomplishment. The only thing that made him happier was... yep, there she was, walking toward him. Gone were her twentieth-century clothes; instead, they both wore nondescript tunics and pants—or shorts—in muted colors. Still, hers outlined every curve, including the bump of her stomach. *Thank you, God.*

*You're welcome, son.*

When Alisha reached him, she slid her arm around his waist and leaned into him. He loved that gesture of intimacy and need. David had been amazed at the change in her since they returned to her time period. She'd become more relaxed, more Zen. He attributed much of it to her ability to be outside here, as well as being back in her element.

"So, what do you think of your handiwork, Rev?" she asked, gesturing at the structure.

"The first church in centuries. I'm thrilled."

Immediately after their return to 2514, the Guardians had called David to meet with them. They'd outlined how they thought David could contribute to their society by seeking out the pockets of religious folk that had sprung up all over the country. They wanted him to encourage the study and learning about God. Because of this, Alisha and David had settled in a four-room *dwelling* near the largest potential con-gregation that had made the most significant progress.

Alisha smiled. "Soon, you'll get to preach in a real house of God," she added.

"You know what I like best about this?" He drew her even closer. "That in this society, all believers come together, regardless of what Supreme Being they follow."

"I agree. No sectarianism. At least, not yet." She kissed his cheek. "Happy Anniversary, by the way."

He cocked his head.

"We've been in my time for a year."

"Ah. Smartest decision I ever made." David had found when he came to this time period that all he really needed in life was God and Alisha. Both were here.

Shading her eyes, she looked up. "I love it when the sun appears."

That didn't happen regularly because, the scientists thought, there had been some permanent damage to the atmosphere in the years of carbon emissions. Though they had day and night now, they never knew when they would be graced by the big yellow sphere's presence. Society had learned its lesson, but not in time.

A man approached David. "Good morning, Reverend." The Guardians hadn't kept David's identity a secret. It had been publicized that he came from the past. Since the research on time travel and the mechanisms to backtrack or project had been destroyed, there was no worry that a rogue member of society would travel to the past and change it.

"Hello, Ezekiel." Ezekiel was one of the mainstays of this community of believers. The man held up a chip, which looked like a flash drive. "This just came for you."

"For me?"

"Both of you. I'm supposed to say, 'Happy First Year.'"

Alisha took the drive. "Let's go sit over there and look at it."

The table was made of synthetics but the benches conformed, which David adored. Alisha pulled out her PDA, aka a hand-held computeller, and inserted the device. Rhea's face came on screen. "Hello, you two. My gift for you on this special revolution is something to celebrate the completion of the first church in our time. As you know, the history chips have been secured in a safe place and aren't accessible to the public. But I wanted you to see a snippet of the 3.0 version."

"I'm surprised she'd send us a history chip." Alisha wondered aloud. "The Guardians were still deciding whether to keep them for posterity or to destroy such contradictory information."

"I've indicated where you should start," Rhea said. "Enjoy!"

"I have a strange feeling about this." Alisha fingered the synthetic aluminum. In an odd twist of fate, she'd become more sensitive to things and people since she returned. Rhea suggested it was a way of balancing the universe since Celeste had left them. Thoughts of her friends saddened her as they usually did, even after being separated for a year.

They found the marked place on the chip and started it there. Alisha gasped. "David, it's the twenty-first century records."

"I see, love."

The computeller spun its tale. Her friends came on screen, smiling, at a picnic, and Alisha's heart kicked in her chest. Celeste held a baby. He had blond hair like the other Lansing children's, but eyes like — amazingly — Alisha's. "He's beautiful. They only had one child, I guess."

"They have four," David corrected.

The chip showed footage of David Law Lansing growing up, starring at sporting events and attending college. "Harvard," David said. "Pretty megadamn good."

A transcript came on. Alisha remarked, "He graduated summa cum laude. And—oh, no—he went into politics!"

David began to chuckle. "He did more than that." He nodded to the swearing-in ceremony. "He became president of the United States in the middle of the century."

A man on screen remarked that his acute sensitivity and ability to see others' points of view had brought this day about.

"Oh, dear Lord in heaven, Celi's child is a sensitive." That made them both smile.

More footage now. "Oh, look David, he had youngers. Five of them."

Named David, Dorian, Jess, Helen, and, of course, Alisha. "How like Celi to talk her son into naming them after us."

"Additional information on other Lansing children," the computeller spoke as different images came on the screen. "Stepdaughter Madison winning the Nobel Peace Prize for her research on safe and effective birth control." The chip showed a totally grown-up Maddy, receiving her award.

Alisha gasped. "Oh, she dedicated it to her father."

Next, a man in a white coat smiled at the camera. "Cody Lansing stands before his twentieth location of *Bruiser's*, his multibillion dollar company of play centers for dogs. He's joined by his brother, Jon"—now a book came on screen—"who wrote the enduring novel for teens about a stepmom and how she changed a family's life."

Tears sprang to Alisha's eyes. Though people leaked them now, only since her pregnancy began had she been so emotional.

"Are you all right?" David laid a hand on her belly. "Maybe we should wait to watch the rest."

"Are you kidding? I want to know about Dorian's family."

They asked for that information. Once again, the computeller revealed her friends' lives. A picture of Jess, looking much like when they left him, appeared. "Jess Cromwell, researcher on carbon emissions, turns his latest project over to his daughter Jessica." Another video of Jessica alone, older, accepting a Pulitzer Prize for her writings on the history of pollution and why man should take steps to eradicate it. She smiled and thanked her father, who had just died at the age of ninety-eight, for his mentorship.

"They lived long and healthy lives."

"We knew we were successful." Alisha grinned. "But not how much." She addressed the machine again. "Report on Lucas Cromwell."

The computeller hummed. "Lucas Cromwell…"

"Look at that," David pointed out.

"Wow, he was offered the position of New York City Police Chief. He turned it down!"

"I wonder why."

Call up information on Dorian Masters from the same era. "Dorian Masters set up an empire of fitness salons nationwide that eventually spread to Europe. Her efforts to fight obesity were lauded by the president, especially after the number of overweight people reached seventy percent of the population."

"Did Luke help her?" David asked.

"Lucas Cromwell raised four children."

"Luke became a stay-at-home dad?" Alisha laughed heartily. "I wouldn't have guessed he had it in him."

"She had twins," David commented. "Two sets. How cool."

"No thanks," Alisha complained, patting her belly. "I'll take mine one at a time." She listened further. "The children became involved in the fitness studios, bringing them to new levels. Oh, one played football."

David laughed. "Hah! I knew that game would last for a while." Few athletics remained from the twentieth century, but new ones had sprung up. He and Alisha had played a version of racquetball and bike racing.

"I wonder what our baby will do, Lisha. Their kids were so successful."

"I hope he carries on our work. Did you notice how closely connected our friends' youngers are to their parents' professions?"

"Maybe by the time this one gets to be an adult, there will be more churches."

"There will always be more churches." Funny, Alisha was certain of that and totally accepting of it.

When the recording ended, David took her hand. "Viewing this made you sad."

"It's a good sad, though, to know what wonderful lives they all led. It's just hard to believe that it happened centuries ago." She yawned.

"Let's get you home. A nap is in order."

"Hmm, my favorite time in the day."

"Yeah, woman, I love being your sleeping pill."

"Music to my mouth."

"To your ears, love."

"Whatever." Both laughed.

In the still-shining sunlight, with arms around each other, David and Alisha walked to the mass-transport stop, waited with the others, and boarded. As it lifted off the ground, and Alisha saw the grass and trees recede, she breathed a sigh of contentment. *Thank you.*

God didn't answer anymore as God used to, but the swell of well-being and the rightness of her life was enough. Alisha lay her head on David's shoulder, her hand on her belly and closed her eyes. Since she'd returned from 2014, she'd experienced optimism about this strange, but wonderful, new world.

And as their faces, as she'd seen them on the chips, swam before her, Alisha knew Celeste and Dorian would be happy for her.

• • •

For notification of Kathryn's new work and information about her books, be sure to sign up for her newsletter at http://on.fb.me/12dhOtc.

If you liked ANOTHER TIME, you might want to post a review of it at amzn.to/192GsjR

Visit or Contact Kathryn at
    www.kathrynshay.com
    www.facebook.com/kathrynshay
    www.twitter.com/KShayAuthor
    http://pinterest.com/kathrynshay/

# AUTHOR'S NOTE

WELCOME TO BOOK three my new series, Portals of Time. This trilogy has been a labor of love for me as I've always been a science fiction/time travel aficionado. But since my first love is romance, there never seemed to be an opportunity to combine the two genres until now. I came up with the original concept for the trilogy years ago, and at last it's come to fruition. Since all the stories take place in the present, I think I was able to keep the books classic Kathryn Shay with a twist. I thoroughly enjoyed creating the new world of the future, playing around with language, and at the same time building a great romance and saying something important about society.

ANOTHER TIME was perhaps the most difficult of the three to write because, honestly, I didn't know what the storyline would be until I wrote the drafts of the first two. But what a story it turned out to be. Could David have been any more adorable? And didn't you enjoy seeing Alisha fall in love with him? One of my favorite scenes in the book was the "practice kissing" scene. I laughed out loud as I wrote it. And I'm not sure if you could tell, but I wasn't sure Alisha made the right decision to pursue the identity of the arsonist.

Probably the best part of the trilogy is what I hope was the unexpected epilogue. It was a delight for me to write and I hope it was fun for you to read.

I hope you didn't miss the first, but if you did, please make sure you catch up with JUST IN TIME and PERFECT TIMING.

Best,

Kathy Shay

www.ingramcontent.com/pod-product-compliance
Lightning Source LLC
Chambersburg PA
CBHW022000170626
46808CB00001B/237